ALSO BY SOLOMON SACKITEY

A Sea of Plight and Pure Joy of the GOLD COAST BOY:
A journey from home to the top of the coconut tree and beyond

(Written under the pen name Bwana Awetse). An inspirational story of resilience in the face of common life situations that people face, such as impediments encountered at school, in sports, in social life, and even at the workplace. Such impediments can be devastatingly ugly but can also uncover the gold and diamonds of sustainable faith in the reader and listener.

ROADMAP

You can never predict what happens on a journey, an errand, a commute, or a sightseeing tour. *Roadmap* serves as your guide through the circumstances encountered in *Circumstances*. It explains basic terminologies and the separation of fiction from nonfiction, while stimulating and attracting a wide range of perspectives on various episodes and themes. Furthermore, it asks questions to illuminate discussions on multiple interesting subjects. Additionally, *Roadmap* provides rudimentary elements of teletourism or virtual tourism to enable "visiting" global tourist attraction centers even in the midst of worldwide public health threats or other catastrophes where countless transportation systems, among other things, are subjected to major embargoes.

CIRCUMSTANCES

SOLOMON SACKITEY

GCB Books

Reading nourishes the mind, soul, society and the future.
Read more, pray more

GCB Books, Frederick, MD, United States of America

ISBN: 9781733379045

Library of Congress Control Number: 2020920087

This book is a coming-of-age work of fiction comprising elements of nonfiction, science fiction, fantasy, romance and adventure inspired by real-life events. The characters, organizations, locations, names, businesses, institutions, incidents, and events, among other things portrayed, are fictitious or used fictitiously. Any similarity to locales, events, or real individuals (living or not) is entirely coincidental or used to fortify the momentum on capacity development.

Disclaimer: Among other things, this book is not intended to provide medical advice, diagnosis, treatment, or any professional advice related to any other industry or sector in any way. Details about regulatory procedures, scientific and technical products, services or processes are beyond the scope of this book. Products and literature cited are for educational purposes only and do not necessarily reflect any and all forms of approval, integrity or endorsement. All website addresses provided are for further reading and knowledge enhancement purposes. There is no conflict of interest whatsoever with reference to the copyright owners of listed websites, organizations, institutions and other resources. Citing these weblinks is not an endorsement, approval, validation of integrity, support, or the like whatsoever. There is no guarantee that website links listed will last indefinitely or work at all after the dates retrieved. Readers are advised to do their own research or due diligence pertaining to the subject matter of interest should the links not function or have any issues. In addition, patrons of these websites are advised to address concerns with the copyright owners directly.

References to the Christian and Muslim religions in this story are not intended to disrespect or disregard any and/or all other religions or non religious beliefs. Biblical verses referenced in this story are not direct quotations from any version of the Bible, but are synopses of verses that could be found in various versions of the Word of God (the Bible).

Discretion: This book may contain material(s) or scenarios that may not be appropriate for everybody. Discretionary decision-making is advised.

CONTENTS

DEDICATION

This book is dedicated to my lovely children, beloved parents, relatives and exceptional mentors, friends, loved ones, and well-wishers who contributed in various ways to making this title a reality.

You all have secured special places in my heart.

Cheers and may God bless you till the end of life.

Continue to read more and pray more.

ABOUT THE BOOK

Pursuing lifetime dreams can be short and smooth sailing for some people. For others, the journey can be tall, long, shallow, deep, treacherously devastating, and humbling with widespread memory lanes. Inspired by real-life events, *Circumstances* traces the paths taken in combing the earth with a toothpick in order to accomplish a dream. Gold Coast Boy undertakes a series of expeditions in his newly invented, mythical biomolecular submarine (Chimeric) that operates on land, in the air, or undersea and can shrink or expand. The breathtaking explorations on four continents, the unique characteristics of each journey, and the circumstances surrounding his life are apt for the reader and listener to discover. Find out for yourself in this NextGen Literature filled with adventures, romance, and family drama, along with the Theology of Genetic Engineering, the biorobotics revolution, humility, the Next Generation Search and Rescue Mission (NextGen SRM), the Infectious Earth Destroyer

(IED)—a rare nanorganism from outer space invading the earth—the global bio civil war (World War III), and more encounters that fill the Chimeric's voyages.

ABOUT THE AUTHOR

Solomon Sackitey earned a Bachelor of Science degree in Biochemistry at Iowa State University and a Master of Science degree in Regulatory Affairs for Drugs, Biologics, and Medical Devices at Northeastern University both in the United States. His professional experience includes serving as a Research Scientist engaged in biotechnology-based human immunodeficiency virus (HIV) Vaccines Research and Development. He also served as a Laboratory Logistics Director involved in coordinating the 2009 novel Influenza A (H1N1) virus (swine flu) pandemic clinical specimen testing in collaboration with the World Health Organization/U.S. Centers for Disease Control and Prevention. A teacher, learner, and loving family man, he is a passionate volunteer as well. He is the recipient of international and domestic awards including a United Nations Online Volunteer of the Year award for creating emergency preparedness initiatives when he volunteered at DatelineHealthAfrica to combat the 2005 highly pathogenic Avian Influenza (H5N1) virus (bird flu) in Africa, HIV DNA Vaccines Team of the Year award at one of the world's best pharmaceutical companies, and Regulatory Affairs Global Leadership award from a prominent innovative pharmaceutical regulatory professionals organization. Awarded two United States patents, Solomon is also the author of *A Sea of Plight and Pure Joy of the Gold Coast Boy* (written under the pen name Bwana Awetse), and *Roadmap.* As a contributing author, he wrote for the *PRESEC-Legon Senior High School Magazine, Iowa Agriculturist,* and the *Iowa State Daily.*

PRELUDE

Seven years and nine months after the first segment of pursuing his dream to find a long-lost friend, Gold Coast Boy (GCB) undertakes multiple search missions.

In *A Sea of Plight and Pure Joy of the Gold Coast Boy* which precedes *Circumstances*, the young boy was engaged in looking for Ibrahim whose controversial deportation from Ghana in the 1960s highlighted astonishing political myopia and the threat to the country's socioeconomic stability.

Circumstances explores the paths Gold Coast Boy takes through traveling in a bio civil war era after gaining revitalized assurances of finding his friend on planet earth. He pursues his goal come hell, the threat of a global bio civil war (World War III) between humans and nanorganisms spearheaded by Infectious Earth Destroyer (IED).

Additionally, he defies blazing heat waves, volcanoes, tornadoes, torpedoes, resurrected dodoes, dense smog, and fog. He is not intimidated by any bad omen, hurricanes, or snow mixed with sleet, and any other disasters. The reader is cautioned not to confuse the IED disease with the Intermittent Explosive Disorder or IED disease reported in the healthcare media.

Everywhere he finds himself in the world, Gold Coast Boy keeps looking through the eyes of a thirty-two dimensional (32D) super-ultrasonic high definition telescope for his friend. He never gets tired of doing so.

NEXT GENERATION SEARCH AND RESCUE MISSION (NEXTGEN SRM)

Expanded search, biorobotics, and bioQnS Detective

Starting from Africa in the former British colony of the Gold Coast (now called Ghana), which is situated off the coast of the Gulf of Guinea, the Gold Coast Boy's exploratory second segment progresses through Europe, Asia, and North America.

During his visit to Ahmadu Bello University (ABU) in Samaru, Zaria, Nigeria years ago, Gold Coast Boy created Genetically Modified (GM) ultra-illuminant coconut trees which served as major sources of electricity predominantly in Africa. On his return to Ghana, he and his team of the Golden Coconut Girls (GCGs) invent at the Asesewa Biotechnology Center of Excellence (ABCE) a rare and

1

unique mode of transportation—the biomolecular submarine system known as Chimeric.

Years later, they develop a Rotator palindromic biorobot, and a mobile, quick, and sensitive detector (bioQnS Detective).

The Rotator palindromic biorobot detects life-threatening biological agents in the environment and destroys them.

The bioQnS Detective helps in the DNA sequence-specific identification of multiple pathogenic agents including the Infectious Earth Destroyer disease in humans, animals, and plants in a single test. This mythical test kit comes with the appropriate IED DNA antibodies or those of the other agents and DNA probes labeled with fluorescent light beams. Test results become available seventy-nine seconds after obtaining a clinical specimen. The tiny device, which is one-quarter the size of a credit card, has the capability to detect one thousand different pathological bioagents in a single test run and can be adapted to test seventy-nine thousand bioagents when needed.

The innovative mystical transportation system created from amphibious chimeric animals, plant and mechanical materials navigates in the air, on the road, undersea, or on the surface of the ocean. It serves as his major means of travel in this multicontinental hunt.

Above all, the Chimeric, Rotator palindromic biorobot, and bioQnS Detective inventions build the foundation for addressing evolving innovations in biorobotics and the rapid detection of biological materials that could threaten the life of human beings.

····· •••••••@••••••·····

In the land-navigation mode where traffic is congested and at a long standstill, it can undergo a mutation that enables it to fly over all other vehicles.

The air-navigation mode is activated through a different kind of mutation.

Another manipulation makes it operate in the submarine or undersea navigation style.

···· ••••••@••••••·····

After gaining biosafety and regulatory clearance from the Ghana Health Regulatory Administration (GHRAd), the International Biotechnology Standards Convention, (IBSC), the Worldwide Environmental Health Agency (WEHA) and the Global Union of Biomarine and Bioaeronautics Regulatory

Authorities (GUBBRA) for the Chimeric, bioQnS Detective, and the Rotator palindromic biorobot, Gold Coast Boy now embarks on his next four-continent mission in search of Ibrahim who got separated from him during his teens because of political turbulence in the 1960s and the 1970s in Ghana throughout the reigns of the Help Yourself (HY) government and military rulers.

* * * * * * * * ● ● ● ● ● ● ● ● ● ● ● ● ● ● * *

Family drama and the Theology of Genetic Engineering (GE)

The New Year brings new hopes, blessings, and aspirations.

On New Year's Day, Gold Coast Boy's intended brief family meeting at Asesewa to seek approval and blessings for his journey turns into a huge drama.

Before engaging the attention of his family and extended relatives, Gold Coast Boy and his mother, Mrs. Merry Oleman, arrange a secret mother-and-son consultation to discuss travel plans in connection with hunting for Ibrahim.

He knocks on his mom's door around 3:00 a.m. and finds his poor old mother still awake.

"Mom, I love you. I couldn't sleep all night. My brain kept tossing me up and down and left to right, and had me doing backward somersaults like a drunken bull. I gave our discussion last night serious thought, and I have decided to move forward chasing my dreams. I will go without committing myself to a sweetheart, and you who will not see me for an unspecified length of time.

"My precious mother, I respect your views and concerns about me. I assure you I will be fine. I shall return, and you will find me a lovely lady with the heart of gold, diamonds, and everlasting faith when I return," Gold Coast Boy promises with the determination of a veteran fighter pilot eager for victory on a tough mission.

"My dear son, if this is your wish, I will accept it, but let me discuss it with your father and let you know what he says. Cool?"

"Haha-haa, Mom. Where did you learn this 'cool' language from?"

They both laugh and embrace.

"Hold my hands, my son, and we pray over it."

Gold Coast Boy goes back to his room.

At the 4:00 a.m. family meeting on New Year's Day, Gold Coast Boy tells everyone, "The journey continues."

"My son, I am concerned that at twenty-two years old, you are still not married, and you are going away again," Mrs. Oleman says, acting surprised while placing her hands gently on Gold Coast Boy's right shoulder.

"Only God knows how long you will be gone. Son, think about it overnight and let me know what you want to do," she counsels him.

"Calm down, Mom. I am only twenty-two years old. I am still young. Allow me to pursue the mountain of dreams that I have," Gold Coast Boy acts in a similar fashion as his mother in order to keep their prior secret discussions intact.

Gold Coast Boy's younger brother, Teye, hides a cough and interrupts the conversation by saying, "Twenty-two years is not young. You are an old man. You better get married and take your wife along with you. Don't behave like some guys who marry and leave their wives behind only to come back to see them being other men's wives, haha, haaa.

"Don't get me wrong though. I know all women are not the same."

Mercy jumps in. "Hey, hey, hey! Hold it right there, young boy. Stop pretending to be smart. I know several men whose wives are living abroad. Can you guess what goes on while these women are away? I bet you wouldn't be able to guess, dunderhead! A mountain of the men impregnate a whole bunch of girls."

Mrs. Oleman listens spellbound.

"Lord, have mercy," Mercy prays for peace and harmony between her and Teye.

The articulate argumentations and gender fights between these special friends do not seem to be ending.

"That is a good point. The family should arrange a marriage for him," says Noble, a family friend and an advocate for peace.

"I will take care of this arranged family marriage at the appropriate time," Mrs. Oleman intervenes.

· · · · · · · · · · ◉ ● ● ● ● ● ● · · · · · ·

"What journey? Is there something I should know about?" the elderly computer-brained Gold Coast Boy's father, whose new name is Mr. Stout Daniel Oleman (Oleman), asks curiously.

"Dad, do you remember that seven years and nine months ago I went to look for my childhood friend in Nigeria but never found him? Instead, I came back with new business ideas which ended up with the creation of genetically modified coconut trees that helped to solve the electricity menace?"

"Oh yes, son. I do remember every detail about that adventurous trip," recollects Oleman.

Baffled, Oleman queries, "Oh my son Gold Coast Boy, would you risk your life taking years of globe-trotting to look for a missing childhood friend amidst all the catastrophic immigration issues, terrorism calamities, nanorganism versus humans civil wars, and the devastatingly horrific natural disasters going on around the world?"

With authority and fatherly love, Oleman enquires from his son, "So, where are you going this time, my main man? Please, don't tell me you are going to Nigeria again with all the terrorist attacks going on in that country.

"Remember you nearly lost your life during a student-military confrontation at ABU in the past?"

"Oh, man, Dad, you have an archaeological memory. The terrorist activities in Nigeria were aimed at girls and young women. I am a man and Ibrahim is a man."

"On this new journey, my son, the air waves are now vibrating vigorously with news about the previously unknown nanorganism. This nanorganism has recently been identified as the Infectious Earth Destroyer or IED that causes the contagious disease known as the IED disease.

"This invasion has resulted in the IED *Global Bio Civil War*, which decorated war veterans refer to as World War III."

"This is a scary major global health concern, Dad".

"Yes, it is. Information about this 'civil war' is as perplexing and camouflaging as its origin, with various sources postulating a series of theories. Lessons from this tragedy would likely never, ever be forgotten because it is perhaps the most dreadful cataclysmic civil war the world will ever see.

"It is impossible to predict what a traveler encounters at any time during a journey. Son, be careful, well prepared and proactive. Stay up to date with public health and travel advisories when you travel.

"Though you should always comply with safety rules, don't be too much alarmed by IED test results or data as some outmoded and inferior test methods may be used. A person may be reported as having the disease when, as a matter of fact, that individual does not have it. Similarly, an individual who may not have the disease may be reported as having it. These false-positive and false-negative test results can be common. Quite a good number of data can be exaggerated to seek public attention and empathy. Regulators and renowned public health experts can be so confused that they may not be in a position to provide clear, unambiguous, reliable regulations and guidelines.

"This is a time to fortify your faith in God and recite the ancestral protection enshrined in the Afadjato chant more religiously. Faith is the motivation for strength, protection, guidance, reliance, confidence and sustenance for achieving perceived unachievables or for building upon trust."

Being proactive, Gold Coast Boy prepares for border closures, biological warfare issues and opens up to the realities and dangers of explorations. He and his entourage carry tons of face masks, gloves, respirators, sanitizers and other personal protective equipment (PPE) for their own use and for donation to the masses everywhere they find themselves. They also donate bioQnS Detective test kits approved for home use following regulatory approvals by global regulatory authorities. Even at locations where there are no reported IED cases, PPE and bioQnS Detective test kits are supplied by Gold Coast Boy free of charge to help contain the blowout of the IED disease pandemonium.

"We will be safe, Dad," Gold Coast Boy assures his old man.

To support his assurance, he hammers in the miracles of DNA technology, biorobotics; above all, God's creation and giving humankind the gift to have dominion over all creatures on earth.

"Be forewarned, IED nanorganism and your allies. With our biotechnology weapons and artillery, we are ready to crush you in the air, on the land, beneath, and on the surface of the seas following the precision and surveillance mechanism of our biorobots technology which never fails. These robots never miss their targets day or night and in between. Under the specialized directions of esteemed combat Air Force pilot Sharon Haron and Marine elite submarine war veteran Regina MacStinard, you will be destroyed using additional capabilities in Rotator palindromic biorobot which detects enemy targets in seventy-nine seconds and destroys them in seventy-nine seconds."

"Really, my son?"

"The biorobotics revolution also promises to conquer the nanorganism's kingdoms and their threats to humanity. With these tools, their entire dominium can get invaded, their genes get rearranged and edited, and IED or any nanorganism is no longer capable of being an infectious pathogen."

Oleman reiterates the horrific nature of this IED Global Bio civil War: "Son, again, be careful, prepared, and proactive. Stay up to date on public health and travel advisories when you travel.

"In spite of the world's superpower nations boasting of their artillery, nuclear arms, World Wars I and II experiences in addition to their progress in space technologies, the IED has the potential of virtually making all countries kneel down before it or fall flat on their faces for not knowing exactly how to develop a safe and effective strategy to wipe off the nanorganism from the earth before it makes human beings extinct.

"In effect, nanorganisms appear to be exerting their supremacy over humans as they seem to be ruling the world. That is how serious the situation can get this time around."

Mrs. Oleman says, "There are opportunities and disadvantages of the IED civil war. Dear family members, please, recollect that technology innovations and God's powers make all things possible.

"The IED civil war has the ability to elevate the advancements of DNA technology as a whole with special reference to gene editing prowess and DNA testing. The bio civil war has the capability of making medical intervention more accessible and affordable through regulated and approved telemedicine—remote medical practices whereby patients can get consultations from any location around the globe without having to be physically present at any medical facilities."

"Furthermore, this civil war is predicted to make new drug research and developments much cheaper and faster while manufacturing and quality assessments among several industries in the future can be done remotely through the use of biorobotics and all other approved robots," says Gold Coast Boy.

"The bio civil war can also positively impact education, work, conferences, festivals, and, as a matter of fact, virtually all industries through remote capabilities. On the other hand, it can bring catastrophic economic, social and environmental disasters of astronomic proportions," adds Mercy.

Teye vehemently disputes all these forward-looking claims. "Wait a minute, everyone! How on earth could this bio civil war add any value to humanity or animal welfare when lives are being destroyed? How could talents driving the biotechnology, information technology, pharmaceutical, business, education, agriculture, and health sectors, for example, be dying around the universe and you view this danger as a blessing? How could killing of God's creations be an opportunity? That is an abominable sin.

"People are losing their livelihoods, families and friends too. Some animals in the zoos are now crying for the end of lockdowns or restrictions on movements of people and business operations, so that they can enjoy the companies of visitors." Teye reminds everybody of their Christian training, animal welfare rights, family and religious values.

What are your views on this global bio civil war debate?

· · · · · · · · · · ● · · · · · · · · · ·

Back to the Asesewa family meeting, Mrs. Oleman says in apparent support of the pursuit of Gold Coast Boy's visions: "First of all, my dear husband, as you already know, for some people, the journey for accomplishing their dreams is short. For others, it is a long journey that can span decades."

Nearly all of the family members nod their heads in agreement with the old lady.

It gets quiet for a moment.

"It seems you have a computer chip planted in your brain, Dad. We need to do genomic sequencing on you to know more about you, your health, longevity, quality of life, and the future of your offspring," articulates Gold Coast Boy.

Teye intrudes after clearing his throat: "You went from genetically engineering coconut trees that marked the beginning of a novel bio-electrification system globally. Now, you are talking about genome sequencing. Then what?

"You are thinking about CRISPR/Cas9 or genome editing, the innovative biomolecular technology that hopes to revolutionize medical intervention and escalate food security?" Teye throws in a topic which cooks a debate on biotechnology; thus, ultimately stimulating the juiciness of family drama and paving the way for a *Theology* of *Genetic Engineering Seminary*.

"Do you mean crispy chicken casserole or crispy chicken with vegetables?" Mercy teases Teye.

Teye exclaims: "Whatever!"

Oleman gets interested in the ongoing arguments about gene editing, genome sequencing, all the chicken casseroles and chicken with vegetables stuff.

In his youthful days, Oleman was a community college biology professor. He lectured on Evolution, and Bible Knowledge.

It is no wonder he gets dragged into this deliberation on modern biology or biotechnology so quickly.

Looking straight in the eyes of Teye, Mercy, Gold Coast Boy, and Rosemary, a co-inventor at ABCE who always refers to Oleman as her mentor and dad, the elderly man minces no words in expressing his objection to the ideas of altering the genetic makeups of any man, woman, child, animal, or creature anywhere, anytime on the planet.

"All these are against the powers of God. Who gave you the audacity to even think about these, oh my children?

"What has happened to all the Christian training you got since the days you were born?"

Gold Coast Boy interjects. "Let me say a little bit about the advantages of biotechnology experiments, Dad. My mobile Chimeric invention is to help humanity. Genome sequencing of the extended family members has a lot of benefits for us and our future generations."

"Bio-tinkmology experiment, you say, brother?" Teye jumps in while Gold Coast Boy tries to throw some light on the technology.

Mercy gets a kick out of Teye's mispronunciation of the word *biotechnology* and cracks a fat joke out of it:

"Hello, Teye, the word is bio-tech-no-lo-gy, not bio-tinkmology. You've got to open your ears and listen to wisdom when people are talking. Let them finish what they have to say before you distract them, boy."

Teye swipes an ugly look at her.

Gold Coast Boy continues with his explanation.

"The future ushers in bright prospects for us to be able to identify and treat heritable or genetic diseases based on these tests."

Deriving motivation from former American President John F. Kennedy's (JFK's) quote "Change is the law of life. And those who look only to the past or present are certain to miss the future" Gold Coast Boy says, "If you dwell on yesterday, you will not know today. If you dwell on today, you have no knowledge of yesterday. If you dwell on today and yesterday, you are surely going to miss tomorrow.

"Change is inevitable and a necessary event. Innovation springs out of change, knowledge of events and activities of yesterday, today, and sticking your neck, heart, soul and mind into tomorrow.

"Yesterday, today and tomorrow—the past, present, and the future—we cannot live without."

$$\cdots \circ \circ \circ \circ \bullet \bullet \bullet \bullet \bullet \circledcirc \bullet \bullet \bullet \bullet \circ \circ \circ \cdots$$

Gold Coast Boy stays focused confidently and convincingly on imparting his biotechnology knowledge to the family.

"Sequencing and cultivating our family genetic tree can provide clues on the identification and treatment options for addressing health issues in a family that keeps growing as large as ours.

"The family DNA tree can also lead to the prevention of marriages of couples that are biologically related. In other words, we can use DNA tests as evidence to say, hey, a brother and a sister from the Oleman big family, living in different parts of the country or in different parts of the world who have not met for years cannot get married because of their closely related genetic makeups. They could be amplifying an inherited disease."

Oleman asks, "Where did you learn all these from, my son?"

"That's not all, Dad, and all of you. DNA tests can be used to set free an innocent person who is sent to jail by matching his or her DNA with that of samples taken as evidence from the crime scene so long as those specimens are collected under strict legal and ethical supervision. Emphatically, no trading of one person's DNA with another person's, intentionally or otherwise.

"DNA can also be used to determine the biological father of a child in paternity disputes."

"This brother of mine is a professor," Teye jokes.

Gold Coast Boy continues his speech. "We could also use DNA tests to easily find blood relatives to donate organs to solve a relative's health condition and a whole lot of other things.

"There will no longer be the need to curse at the woman or the man in the neighborhood whose new-borns die during birth or right after birth. Sickle cell disease will be a thing of the past," I assure you.

"How can you be so sure about this, Professor? Are you a prophet or you are speaking in parables?" Teye abruptly cuts in again.

Gold Coast Boy goes on with his thought-challenging speech: "Sorcery and the curse from the psychic practice involving witchcraft or *juju* as we call it in Africa, will no longer be rumor mongering activities in the community to stigmatize women who are wrongly chastised as solely responsible for not being capable of bearing children due to their infertility problems."

"You hear that, Mercy?" Teye points his left fingers at Mercy whilst looking away.

As Mercy also raises her left arm to whack Teye, Oleman tries to intercept her. In the ensuing scuffle, Oleman falls on the sofa.

There is no casualty. Thank God.

In moving forward with his speech to make a case for biotechnology, Gold Coast Boy cautions, "Think about all these. There are numerous benefits and challenges of family DNA tree planting.

"Some of the risks of biotechnology include abuse motivated by self-aggrandizement. Always bear in mind that when making decisions, you should consider the fact that benefits always outweigh the risks."

The family disperses for a hot chocolate and tea break.

* * * * * * * * * ● * * * * * * * * * *

Rosemary takes the spotlight following the short recess.

"Dad, I appreciate your concerns about the ethical and religious issues you brought up in this grossly misunderstood topic of genetic engineering.

"I will lead an effort for the Ghana government to draft and lay down the regulatory framework for more dynamic policy-making machinery.

"A coalition of the Christian Council of Ghana, Muslim groups, and all interested parties will be motivated to illuminate the perceptions on biotechnology so as to make everyone build their knowledge base about the benefits, challenges, misconceptions, fears, and opportunities for innovating the future of health, food security, and our environment." Rosemary joins the discussion of issues on biotechnology.

· · · · · · ● ● ● ● ◉ ● ● ● ● ● · · · ·

"By the way, is biotechnology stated anywhere in the Bible at all?" Teye asks, further inflaming the biotechnology controversy and heightening curiosity about genetic modifications.

"Oh yes, my son," Mrs. Oleman quickly answers. "You remember the Bible is essentially saying in Leviticus 19:19 that cattle shall breed with cattle only? This is basically cautioning us about mixing unrelated genes. For example, we should not allow cattle genes to be transferred into dogs."

Gold Coast Boy jumps in to further contribute to the reflections on biotechnology as it is one of his motivations for doing what he has been doing.

"But a strong case is established to support genetic alteration or biotechnology in the Bible as recorded in Genesis 1:26-27, where God said He has given humankind power over the livestock, fish, and all creatures on the earth.

"What we learn from this is that God has given us humans the privilege to use these creatures, plants, and animals for purposes of solving their health problems, for example. This can include tinkering with their genes to solve their health problems and meet their nutritional needs.

"God has given humanity, male and female, the gift that He entrusted in human beings to use these creatures, living things, and possibly nonliving things to make whatever they can as long as they are made in His image or in a way that pleases Him.

"Therefore, why should anybody be concerned if a man or woman uses God's freely given gift for creating or modifying a living organism, a nonliving organism, or synthetic materials to solve problems facing the earth's inhabitants?

"After all, plant scientists including Nobel Prize winner Barbara MacClintock, and Donald S. Robertson, among other scientists have shown that genetic engineering occurs naturally. You may have heard of or read about *Jumping Genes* or transposable elements which are pieces of DNA that jump from one place to another within the genome of living organisms like bacteria, plants, animals, viruses, and humans. So, biotechnology or genetic engineering has been known to humankind for centuries. It is not man-made; it is nothing new. Jumping genes can create mutations or changes in genomes that may be used for various desirable benefits to humanity and the environment. Of course, some mutations may not be beneficial.

"Consider, for example, a transposable element-induced mutation that occurs in the carotenoid genes of corn plants. A mutation such as this can be used to create a vitamin A rice which is not normally present in the native rice plant. This genetically modified rice can provide vitamin A which is a vital nutritional element essential for boosting the immune system.

"When you try to dissuade people from eating a genetically modified agricultural product such as apple, mango, papaya, avocado pear, tomato, roasted goat meat, grilled sheep meat, or barbecued pig, either because you dislike its taste or because you are not used to the 'new' taste, would you rather see people starve or die of hunger and malnutrition?"

"Please, don't point fingers at me. I don't try to deshade nobody, brother," Teye interjects with his mis-pronunciation of the word *dissuade* as '*deshade*'.

Mercy, as usual, wastes no time in responding to Teye. "Hey, Teye, the word is not '*deshade*.' It is dissuade."

"He is not referring to you personally. He is using the word *you* in general terms. That is, *you* as singular and not plural. That means it can apply to anybody.

"Please, chill."

"By the way, what tastes good for one person may be unpleasant for another," Gold Coast Boy moves on with his message.

"Like ethics—taste is like ethics. What may be tasty to one person may not be tasty to another. What may be yummy for someone may be yucky for another person. Similarly, what may be ethical for one individual may not be ethical for another."

"Tasty or not tasty, salivating or not salivating, is tantamount to ethical or not ethical views," Teye concurs with Gold Coast Boy.

"I am proud of you, young man, Gold Coast Boy flatters Teye."

"Maybe, I am wrong. I may be wrong this time," Teye wonders.

"Would you rather have a yummy-tasting grilled chicken salad and goat meat pepper soup for lunch or dinner?" Mercy asks Teye.

"Maybe, for lunch," Teye answers.

Now, on the argumentations about biotechnology in the Bible, Gold Coast Boy clarifies some points in a series of statements.

"What the Theology of Genetic Engineering is preaching through its seminaries is that mankind should use God's freely given genetic gifts to bring salvation to His people while glorifying His holy name.

"My friend Ibrahim, a Muslim, and his Muslim friends also share this Christian philosophy.

"Why would any creature or human being be forced, intimidated, influenced, or threatened to change its, his, or her genetic superiority endowed on it, him, or her by God?

"Forcibly varying God's gifts, such as intelligence or athletic preeminence, without even thinking of the fact that such undesirable medical changes can result in serious side effects is wrong.

"The technologies surrounding genetic engineering should not be feared. It is human beings that you must be afraid of."

"My son, you seem to be swaying my way of thinking in this discussion on modern genetic engineering. Now, I am very interested in hearing why you think humankind must be the culprit instead of the technology," Oleman presses for more clarity.

"This is because some individuals may have no regard to the Laws and Regulations governing, Research and Development, Clinical Trials, Manufacturing and Product Labeling, for example.

"Others may not respect patient privacy rights and protection. Some people may not have a trace of humility embedded in them when harming God's earthly creatures by intentionally misusing or abusing the technologies for the purpose of enriching or making names for themselves.

"In maternity dispute cases, babies can be intentionally or inadvertently swapped at birth making DNA testing results irrelevant.

"In the same way, substituting a man's specimens to be used in DNA analysis can prove the innocent man being responsible for a conception."

At this point, Oleman is bent on bringing the family meeting to a close.

To Gold Coast Boy come words of blessings from the bottom of the heart of a loving dad in what some folks would describe as "A love letter from a Dad to his son":

"You have my blessings, son. Go in peace. But don't stay too long. I don't have much more time to live. I want to see you back before my journey to heaven."

"Thank you, Dad. You have a long time at your disposal before God calls you to heaven for everlasting and peaceful rest. Besides, God has blessed you with the genes that prolong your healthy life on earth. I shall see you back in no time. Rest assured, Dad."

They all say good night and leave for bed.

• • • • • • • • • • ⊛ • • • • • • • • • • •

It is breakfast time at 8:00 a.m. The whole family gets together around the breakfast table. Teye volunteers to say the prayers before they eat.

"Oh God, our Heavenly Father, please join us, make this meal healthy, wholly, and provide for everybody else in this world. Please, make it possible for the sick who cannot eat to be able to eat.

"Some people have the food but they cannot eat for various reasons whilst others don't have any food at all, yet they can eat, and eat, and eat. May you bless the farmers, the chefs, and the eaters including the traveler, my big brother. Amen."

Everyone politely says "Amen" in unison.

The dining room gets so quiet you can hear the steps of an ant tiptoeing around the kitchen table to grab some munchies to eat and some to store for the next day.

Oleman gives his traditional hat, which he inherited from his grandfather, to his son, Gold Coast Boy, as tears keep streaming down his cheeks like the gentle water flowing down the Boti waterfalls in the Eastern Region of Ghana.

In an emotional presentation of a parting gift, Oleman, holding the hat on his heart with his right hand, stammers as he says, "Son, here, take this hat with you and remember us always. It will give you strength anytime you encounter challenges. It will also grant you the courage bestowed on us from our ancestors.

"Whenever the world seems to turn against you, whenever you feel you are moving backward instead of forward, close your eyes briefly and say *resi, resi, lience, lience, resilience, resilience.*

"Then, with your eyes widely opened and looking beyond the skies, you should end up by reciting the Afadjato chant: *Afadjato ooo, Afadjato, Afadjato ooo, Mountain Afadjato, Afadja, Afadja, Afadja.* To sanctify this chant, you must hold the *Ahuja* in your right hand and sing and dance as you point it to heaven and earth followed by clockwise and counterclockwise circular motions before touching your chest or any part of your body with it. This proverbial horsetail is a spiritual medium for enriching blessings, protection and guidance. It also dispels curses. The *Ahuja* is your African ancestral magic wand."

The family agrees for him to go with all of God's protection, blessings, mercies and guidance.

Feeling sad, mom says a brief prayer as she soaks her handkerchief by drying off her tears.

Off he goes.

· · · · · ● ◉ ◉ ⬤ ◉ ◉ ● · · · · ·

Schmoozing

After the family drama, blessings, and advice to go ahead with his travel plans, Gold Coast Boy takes off from Asesewa to Accra with an old friend, Tom Jayson (TJ), in his Chimeric, following the emotional farewell, cheers, and sobbing.

An old, trusted elementary school classmate and friend of both Gold Coast Boy and Ibrahim, TJ, who is now a businessman in Accra, promises he has the network to help locate Ibrahim within a short time.

He offers his old companion to stay with him for as long as it takes to find Ibrahim which he believes should not be longer than a month.

Oh, how some people can change.

As an aspiring mayor of CityLaPaz, a suburb of Accra, TJ needs so much cash to fuel his campaign. His intention is to grab as much money as possible from his old friend, fair or foul. For this, he tries several times to swindle Gold Coast Boy out of thousands of U.S. dollars.

"He is loaded with bags and bags of dollars. Look at that, Dad, your friend owns a personal jet he calls Chimeric," the tall, lanky, and eloquent nineteen-year-old Abigail, who is aptly nicknamed Tsetse Fly, encourages her father to work harder to make some money out of him.

· · · · · · · · · · ● · · · · · · · · · · ·

Careful observation of Abigail's lips when she talks or is silent reveals her moods . When her lips are twisted to the left, that means danger. Lips warped to the right signify good news. Loosened lips mean cooking up some strategy that can be good or evil. Likewise, pay attention to her relatively long and pointed nose, which she uses to sniff out potentially wealthy targets.

· · · · · · · · · ◉ · · · · · · · · · ·

"Good idea, my favorite daughter. But how?"

"Dad, did you tell him he will be staying in your house for free?"

"Not really."

"Great. You've got him, Dad!" she says with excitement as she jumps and raises her hands into the sky.

"Did he ask if you're going to charge him, Dad?"

"Nope."

"Bingo! When he is ready to leave, give him a bill for US$3,000. This is the cost of his accommodation, meals, entertainment, local transportation, rental of high-rise office buildings for meetings with top politicians who have the connections to help locate Ibrahim, and for incidental expenses. It doesn't matter how short or long his stay will be."

"Great. You are so brilliant, Abigail!"

They exchange high fives.

"Abigail, I am always proud of you."

TJ promises his daughter, "When I win this election, you will definitely be appointed the Chief Financial Officer and Secretary-General of the CityLaPaz Mayor's Office."

· · · · · · ● ● ● ◉ ● ● ● · · · · · · ·

A fortnight at TJ's residence is more distressing than what spending quality time with an old friend should be.

Gold Coast Boy decides to move out after putting up with the nuisance of a yellow cat, the size of a ten-year-old bloated pig, as stubborn as a one-legged red mosquito dying of starvation.

At the end of his two-week stay at TJ's, Gold Coast Boy receives a bill for US$10,000.

"What the …. What the heck is this humongous bill for?" Gold Coast Boy asks his friend, looking straight in his eyes with total shock as blazingly sharp as a butcher's knife.

Abigail stands right behind her Dad, resting her v-shaped chin on his right shoulder as her lips are twisted to the left while she peeks at Gold Coast Boy.

Gold Coast Boy takes off to the skies in his Chimeric without a word or a payment in any form.

"Oh, how some people can change. I thought he was still my friend. What happened to the good old days we played football and spent time together as family friends? All these were gone to the winds just like that?" he says to himself.

What is the outcome of TJ's promised networking influence to help find Ibrahim? Nil. Nothing. No success. Just bills.

* * * * * * * * ● ● ● ● ● ● ● * * * * * * *

When TJ re-establishes contacts with Gold Coast Boy a few months later, there is an absolute change of heart.

In their reunification conversation, when asked about his mayoral electoral votes, TJ gets so embarrassed concerning the outcome of the voting.

Garnering some courage, he tells it all: "I got only four votes. Not four percent of the votes. I had only a total of four votes, including my own."

"So sorry you were not elected as you had hoped for," Gold Coast Boy sympathizes with TJ.

"I lost not only my ambition to become the mayor of CityLaPaz, but I lost my children and my wives.

"My first wife Melinda passed away tragically. Abigail, the only child I had with Melinda, was awarded a United Nation's scholarship to do her DPhil in Clinical Psychology at Suthie University in the United Kingdom (UK)."

TJ becomes furious when he hears that after Abigail's studies, she got married without his knowledge to Harry, a British commercial pilot in Manchester.

He misses out on a self-conceived notion of getting a free flight to attend an Afro-Brit wedding and his first-ever stepping into an airplane.

That is enough to mark the beginning of the end of his communications with his so-called favorite child.

"Can you believe, Gold Coast Boy, that Abigail would not even return my calls or reply to my letters?

"That's not only my reward for the deliberate attempts to betray our friendship. It has also been a ploy carefully crafted by Abigail." "Really! So, Abigail strategized all those maneuvers?"

"My second wife, with whom I had five children, has migrated to Dallas, Texas, in the United States with all our five children, following her secret marriage to her high school sweetheart, who had been in America for years. I had no knowledge whatsoever that Ellen and Ishmael had been communicating for a great amount of time.

"Ellen and I didn't even get a divorce when Ishmael filed for papers with the U.S. Embassy in Accra and took all six of them away. "Now I am wondering if I fathered all or some of Ellen's children."

Gold Coast Boy, in an effort to help him with this issue of biological fatherhood determination of the children says, "DNA testing can be the judge in your paternity litigation."

DNA test results afterwards show that only one out of the five children is TJ's biological child. Rumor mongers soon take delight in gossiping about how frequently Ishmael had been visiting Ghana in the past. Mass media outlets also report that Abigail gets caught in human trafficking involving young girls and women.

Poor Abigail. When her chameleon character doesn't help anymore, she ends up serving a five-year jail term in the United Kingdom.

"All my sins against you and other innocent victims have boiled over my dubious pots of evil and spread all over. Kneeling down before you and holding your legs, I can't express how to beg you for forgiveness, Gold Coast Boy, and ask you to take me back as your friend, a genuine friend again."

"Oh, let me think over it and get back to you."

"How long will it take for you to do that? I am all ears."

"Hmm. Am not sure. Allow me some time to discuss it with my parents and some friends. TJ, let me think about your request. Let me hear what they say, alright?"

Five weeks pass by and TJ is still in suspense.

Each week he calls Gold Coast Boy who says he and those whose views he plans on hearing are still thinking about his request.

"Give us some time to think, TJ. I will be getting back to you soon."

"Ok, but how soon?"

"Oh, don't worry. We will weigh the risks and benefits as we consider your case. Please, give us some time to think, TJ. I will be getting back to you soon."

Forty days later.

"After further consideration, praying, and fasting for over fourteen days and fourteen nights, I have decided to forgive you and welcome you back wholeheartedly into our restored friendship, TJ. Friendship is a borderless world and a relationship that is sustainable under any and all circumstances. You are forgiven."

"Awww, thank you, Gold Coast Boy. You have a priceless and unconditional forgiving heart. God bless you for opening your arms to the Immoral friend."

The consequences of scandalous schmoozing are cataclysm, devastation, and alienation but transparency in networking is a joy forever.

· · · · · · ●●●●● ◉ ●●●●● · · · · · ·

Gold Coast Boy's second journey to Nigeria begins in his newly created biomolecular submarine by road from Nima Station in Accra to Ajenkula, a suburb of Lagos. From Ajenkula, he goes to the Lagos bustling suburb of Suru Lere, where he embarks on the next segment of his journey.

First, to Bayero University in the northern Nigerian State of Kano, then back down south to Kaduna State at ABU.

On the 2,000-kilometer (1,242.7-mile) Lagos-Kano trip, he watches various Naijawood movies, including *Erbb, Where Is My Friend* in his satellite television (TV)-equipped Chimeric.

University students versus the military confrontations in Nigeria have been prevalent since his last visit, seven years and nine months ago.

Harassment, torture, and brutality of Ghanaians in Nigeria are not uncommon. The ruling Help Yourself party in Ghana does not do much about the predicament of its citizens.

It comes as no surprise when Nigeria finally deports Ghanaians, apparently in retaliation for Ghana's previous deportation of Nigerians, including those who were born in Ghana and had been living in the country for generations with virtually no place to call home in Nigeria.

* * * * * * * * ● ◉ ● ● ● ● ● ● * * *

When he finds himself sailing in the dark, moving from darkness to the unknown world, Gold Coast Boy persists in searching for his friend. In doing so, he gets the tremor of his life after a near-death encounter with the Nigerian military during a nationwide student-military crisis fueled by increased tuition fees.

Student stipends and some government scholarships are withdrawn. University scholars across the country stage peaceful demonstrations which get ignited into violent protests as the result of a weeklong, curfew imposed across the nation.

On that fateful, bloody day, close to fifteen student demonstrators are killed by the soldiers at the university community where Gold Coast Boy is being accommodated by some Ghanaian Good Samaritans, according to radio, TV, and newspaper reports that Saturday.

He steps out of the university bungalow of his friends, Madam Aminatu, a breastfeeding Nigerian woman, and her husband, Professor Ariksome from Australia, after having lunch with them.

Poor Gold Coast Boy suddenly finds five fully armed and dangerous soldiers within three feet (or a few meters) of him. They instantly command him to raise both of his arms. He obliges immediately without any hesitation but makes a mistake and turns his head to the door in an attempt to quickly jump back into the house.

"If you move, you will be killed. I never miss my targets," one of the armed soldiers guarantees his death as all five of them point their loaded guns at him.

He makes another mistake by smiling at them. He is commanded to kneel down. He complies. As he gets down on his knees with both arms still in the air, one of the soldiers moves closer to him and whips his head severely, with the hook of his belt landing on his right eye. He starts to bleed.

A third soldier goes ahead and uses the barrel of his gun to hit his head, as this soldier feels Gold Coast Boy is making a mockery of them.

Gold Coast Boy is silent.

Everything happens so swiftly that Aminatu's pleading with the soldiers gets drowned in the commotion. Visibly traumatized, she holds her baby by her side as he is busily imbibing his milk for lunch. Aminatu gets on her knees and keeps speaking the Hausa language of the soldiers asking them to spare Gold Coast Boy's life. The baby touches the hearts of the soldiers with his fancy giggling and hand-waving moves.

God intervenes. The military men walk away. Gold Coast Boy is not killed.

* * * * * * * * ● * * * * * * * * * *

Speaking other people's languages can perform mysterious miracles. They hear their languages travelling all over in their hearts, brains, and souls according to the wisdom in the words of former South African President Nelson Mandela when he said, "If you talk to a man in a language he understands, that goes to his head. If you talk to him in his language, that goes to his heart."

* * * * * * * * ● * * * * * * * * * *

Prof. Ariksome fears for his life and continues to hide in the house.

Some people whom Gold Coast Boy thinks are his friends ridicule him when they hear about his encounter with the Nigerian army.

"You, Gold Coast Boy, you have no head at all. You are unemployed. What were you doing out there at the University Housing in this turmoil? Did you not hear the news about the killing of innocent students from Nigeria and foreign countries going on for the past few days?" Ben taunts with a contagious laughter.

Harriett gets back at Ben: "You are the one who has no head at all, Ben. How can you get a job just sitting in the house on your behind and not going out networking?"

Gold Coast Boy stands small. He meditates and asks that Ben be forgiven by God.

There are a few good friends who sympathize with Gold Coast Boy. They bring him sympathy cards and banana tree flowers, which are believed to be endowed with miraculous healing powers from the ancestors.

Emelia asks, "Hey, my friend, what happened to the hat your old man gave you before you left Ghana? It was supposed to get you out of trouble. Remember?"

"Come on, Emelia. Would you have dared to pull the hat out of your pocket under such circumstances? Be nice to the poor boy," Harriett confronts Emelia.

· · · · · · · · · ● ● ● ● · · · · · · · ·

After the soldiers walk away, Aminatu further chants some Hausa words that summon a few brave men and women. These individuals help carry Gold Coast Boy on a Vespa motorbike to the crowded ABU hospital Emergency Room (ER) for treatment.

One of the ladies responding to the chant meant to help save Gold Coast Boy's life, Ms. Abbosey, happens to be a Senior Registered Nurse very well-known at this hospital. She is, however, barred from crossing a demarcated line where patients usually wait for three to four hours before being attended to.

Ms. Abbosey's beauty coupled with her heart-warming smile at the male security guard on duty is so charming that they melt his heart. In conjunction with these enticing physical characteristics and actions, Ms. Abbosey gives the guard a hug as big as an elephant and he falls on the floor.

These actions are enough bribes to allow the security guard to grant Ms. Abbosey permission to register

Gold Coast Boy. Subsequently, a doctor on duty is quickly called in who comes and treats Gold Coast Boy.

This scenario angers other patients and their families who have been waiting for hours without even getting registered or signed in. At the same time, Ms. Abbosey's strategy becomes a huge motivation for the women who have been at the ER for the most part of the day.

A swarm of young women hops on the security guard and gives him kisses and smooching and each one rubs her hands on his head.

He loses his mind. This is a big mess, but several patients get to be registered and treated sooner.

· · · · · · · · · · ● ● ● ● ● ● · · · · · · · ·

Corruption can be really contagious, some people believe.

With no shame or humility, the ER doctors ask the sick patients and family members what they would get in return for helping them out.

"Nothing?" questions Dr. Yaro in disbelief.

"Your protection, long life, and the biggest hugs from God's angels will be yours till you die," a thirteen-year-old girl happily answers Dr. Yaro, who is the head of the ER Department.

He is instantaneously pacified by the teenage girl's answer.

· · · · · · · · ● ◉ ● · · · · · · · · · ·

Just two weeks after Gold Coast Boy's right eye gets healed, he experiences another intervention.

He is offered a job with the International Development Program (IDP) as a Senior Technical Officer in Zaria. He quickly rises through the ranks and becomes a Research Manager in charge of the Pearl Millet and Sorghum Breeding programs in the whole of the West African sub-region, reporting to the African Region Chief Executive Officer, Dr. S. OO.

· · · · · · · · ● ◉ ● · · · · · · · · · ·

Challenges continue crossing the paths of Gold Coast Boy as he pursues his tumultuous mountain of dreams.

The IDP vehicles he has oversight over get stolen one day. This results in a hunt all the way from Kaduna to Lagos, following a fruitless search for the two white Peugeot 505 salon cars in Kaduna, Kaduna State.

Three months after the hunt for the stolen vehicles, Gold Coast Boy gets excited when some mass media professionals he met on his first trip promised they could use their expertise in radio and television advertising to help him quickly find his friend, whom they assured him has been in the country for some time now.

Abiba, Gold Coast Boy's primary liaison in Nigeria, tells him she and her comrades would surely assist him.

"We can help you, *broder, but una glease our pams small, small.*" [This Nigerian pidgin English language translates to "My brother, we can help but you have to give us a little token."]

As a matter of fact, they are asking for a bribe in U.S. dollars.

The conversation in pidgin English escalates: *"Haba, how now? Na mi bi your broder, abi? So, how cum una wan make I glease your pams?"* ["What's going on now? I am your brother, isn't that so? So, how come you want me to grease your palms?"] Gold Coast Boy responds to Abiba, the tall, charming, twenty-two-year-old lady always beaming with smiles.

"You see, normally, we charge our clients heavily to promote them on the airwaves 'live,' but because you are our brother, we are just asking for a token. This token will be shared among *di ogas* who are the big bosses so that things move fast," Abiba justifies the demand for fees.

"How much are we talking?"

"Only US$500."

"Only US$500? *Me, I de cum from Ghana nobi America.*" ["Me, I come from Ghana, not America."]

"*We dey Naira land; not in Dollar land. Wetin now?*" ["We are in Naira land, the land of the Nigerian currency, not the land of the American dollar. What's going on now?"]

"It would normally cost you one thousand dollars, to be honest with you," Gold Coast Boy," Abiba tries to put pressure on him.

"I don't carry cash with me when I travel. Where can I get some dollars to buy?" Gold Coast Boy timidly whispers to Abiba.

Abiba points to some building a walking distance away as she says, "There is a Forex Bureau right around the corner there. Here, follow me. I will take you there."

Gold Coast Boy yields to the swindlers' five hundred dollars "fee" and gives Abiba the amount after the quick trip to the Forex Bureau.

. . . . ● . . . .

Eight o'clock in the morning, the next day.

Abiba and Gold Coast Boy appear at the Kano Super TV-3 Station for a "live" interview in which Gold Coast Boy recounts his story leading to the exile of his friend. He also promises US$500 to anyone whose information could lead to finding his friend.

This "live" TV broadcast turns out to be fake. There are numerous telephone calls from within the TV studio with informants claiming they have found Ibrahim; the friend Gold Coast Boy has been looking for.

In addition to the reward of US$500, some callers are asking to be taken for lunch at the five-star Bagauda Lake Hotel in Kano.

It turns out that these calls are fake and attempts to dupe Gold Coast Boy.

The "Nawa ooo" (Amazing) talk show host on Super TV-3, who promises to provide two copies of the TV recordings, keeps saying, "Oh, trust me, my brother. You do not have to worry. I will give you the tapes soon. My technician is busy with some urgent assignments and he will get to your tapes soon."

The word "soon" has no defined limits in the duper's vocabulary.

This promised tape is never to be made available.

· · · · · · · ● ● ● ● ◉ ● ● ● ● · · · · · ·

The next day, Abiba and Gold Coast Boy go on a 50-kilometer (31.1 mile) ride to KNT 98.6FM Radio Station in Ogina Township, also in Kano State, for a "live" interview.

On their way, they are overtaken by a driver who is in a good mood and enjoying the weather. He raises his left arm and points the three middle fingers at the occupants of Chimeric.

In total dismay, Gold Coast Boy asks, "Hey, what did I do wrong to deserve that driver cursing at me?"

Abiba laughs and says, "That driver was just saying hello. That is a nice gesture in this Nigerian culture. He was not cursing at anybody."

All passengers on board Chimeric laugh so loudly.

"What is culture?" asks Chineke, one of the occupants.

"Good question, Chineke," Abiba compliments her.

In a short discourse by Abiba, she goes, "The meaning of 'culture' is diverse and can vary from region to region or from one geographical area to another.

"Wait a minute. I presume you are not asking about the meaning of *culture* in biology, such as bacterial culture, plant tissue culture, or human or animal tissue cultures, are you, Chineke?"

"Not really, Abiba," answers Chineke.

Abiba proceeds, "So, in plain language, among other things, culture is about:

"Gestures, other verbal and nonverbal communication styles; how males and females interact and how different religious groups and beliefs are perceived;

"How to interrelate with geography, food, fashion, jokes, and looks;

"And diversification, which has the potential to lead to innovation and sticking one's neck out in the future."

"What is culture not about?" Chineke seeks more explanation.

"Contrary to general perspectives, culture is not only about language, food, clothing, facial features, the shape of heads, and physical appearances of people. For instance, it is not about the different ethnic practices between and among:

"Africans—for example, Yoruba, Igbo, and Hausa tribes of Nigeria; Kikuyu, Maasai, and the Kisii of Kenya; Akan, Ga-Adangme, Dagomba, and Ewe people of Ghana; and Zulu, Xhosa, and Venda tribes of South Africa;

"Asians—for example, Bhil and Khasi tribes of India, Yamato and Ainu of Japan;

"Americans—for example, Caucasian and Cherokee;

"Mexicans—for example, Yucatán and Quintana Roo, or many different indigenes around the world," Abiba enlightens Chineke.

Everyone pays rapt attention to Abiba as she further elaborates on cross-cultural awareness:

"Raising the middle finger of the left hand can be insulting in one culture while the same gesture can be pleasing in another.

"It is a cultural norm to remove your shoes or sandals before entering the palace of a chief or a person from a royal family as a sign of respect.

"If you fail to do so, you may get penalized heavily."

"Oh thanks, Abiba. I have always been proud of how high my cultural intelligence is, until today. Now, I have learnt something new."

"I hope you have learnt something new from me too," Gold Coast Boy tells Abiba and the other occupants of Chimeric.

* * * * * * * * ● * * * * * * * * *

After dinner with Abiba's collaborators, TQ Slice, a radio and television personality, and his five team members at another five-star hotel, Abiba and Gold Coast Boy board his Chimeric and head down south to the town of TheTruth in Christar State for a second "live" radio show at the Liberty 69FM radio station.

Preceding the radio interview, Gold Coast Boy, Abiba, and the radio host Adams Crooked make a customary courtesy visit Nicodemously (at night) to the Lead Paramount Chief of Christar State, Rev. Dr. Joe Loyal.

For failure to accompany the visit with imported alcoholic drinks (three bottles each of schnapps and whisky) in addition to a gallon of the locally brewed, high-content alcoholic drink *ogogoro*, Gold Coast Boy and his entourage are fined two cows and two goats for violating cultural formalities.

Moreover, they are each fined a portable air conditioner for not bowing down their heads when greeting the Paramount Chief.

Their handshakes and attempts to hug the Chief are inappropriate.

* * * * * * * * * ● ● ● ● ● ● ● ● ● ● ●

The obstacles in Gold Coast Boy's voyages don't seem to be ending.

It turns out that all the efforts are well orchestrated mass media fraudulent activities.

Abiba, who claims her personnel are all legitimate, vows she will make sure Gold Coast Boy gets copies of the radio and TV recordings. She fails on her promises.

Several months have gone by and Ibrahim's whereabouts are still a mystery. Neither recorded videos nor audio tapes can be obtained as promised by Abiba and her gang.

Gold Coast Boy's collaborators return to their respective towns after the unfruitful visit to the royal palace while he is left alone. He returns to ABU in Zaria.

Several weeks later, a new Nigerian government, the National Alliance in Nigeria (NAIN) comes into power following peaceful democratic elections. Over the past few months since the Forex Bureau scam, NAIN has been engaged in political and economic soul-cleansing operations. After an intensive investigation into the actives of the suspected gangsters, followed by a jury trial, Abiba and her team have been found guilty of various types of fraud and are serving variable prison terms ranging from six months to eight years.

* * * * * * * * *⬤* * * * * * * * *

In a "coughing corpse and the cops" episode, a frustrated and disappointed Gold Coast Boy ends up all by himself again in a desolate Nigerian village called Savage in Mamamdika State where his Chimeric experiences a problem in the navigation control panels around 9:00 p.m. He stands by the roadside hitchhiking nervously, hoping he gets to a nearby town with decent hotel accommodation.

His darkness turns into light, he believes, when he sees a vehicle coming his way. He waves at the driver and the old boneshaker wooden truck carrying two women and the driver stops.

"I have a problem with my vehicle on a journey I have been undertaking in pursuit of my missing childhood friend. I will be glad if you could give me a ride to the nearest town where I can stay overnight," he tells his sad story while pleading with the driver for help.

There is a long calmness. Neither the driver nor the passengers utter a word. The two ladies look at each other's faces, look at the back seats, and stare at Gold Coast Boy.

Kofi, the driver, breaks the silence: "Sir, I do not know how far the nearest town is and I do not know if there are any hotels along the way either."

"Oh no. I just need to get out of here and seek shelter somewhere."

"Sure, if you would not mind the condition this vehicle is in, I guess we can give you a ride to wherever you find a place to spend the night," Kofi says.

"Oh, thank you, thank you so much. You are my saviors. May God bless you all," Gold Coast Boy expresses his gratitude as he climbs into the truck and sits at the back while the two women stare at the dead body wrapped up in a piece of cloth and lying on the floor.

"By the way, is your friend dead or alive?" Kofi asks Gold Coast Boy.

"I am not sure if he is dead or alive, Sir."

"Is your friend a male or female?" one of the women asks.

"A male. His name is IBM alias Ibrahim. Have you heard of a name like that or have you come across a person by that name?"

"Well, he is probably the person lying on the floor behind you, a dead person," Kofi says.

"Oh no, God forbid! Please, don't tell me this is Ibrahim. He should be thirty years by now."

The second lady says, "No, it can't be him. The corpse lying here is that of a nineteen-year-old."

Gold Coast Boy inhales deeply and exhales quickly with relief.

The police patrol riding in an armored Range Rover stops them for a random inspection. Kofi gets pulled out of his bone shaker truck for questioning.

Gold Coast Boy is interrogated. The policemen don't believe him when he says he has no knowledge about the circumstances surrounding the death of the individual in the truck.

Irene and Julia (the two ladies in the boneshaker truck) and Kofi can't fend for Gold Coast Boy when they get interrogated. They say they do not know him.

"Why did you pick a person off the street in the middle of the night when you have no clue about him? Police Officer Jake questions Kofi. "He could have been a criminal," the Officer adds.

"I thought about it for a moment and came to the decision that I can use this situation to demonstrate that humans are capable of doing good to others, even strangers. The good deed that I do to him can come back to me some day," Kofi replies with faith.

"Good, but your safety must always come first," the policeman advises him.

"I trust God has me already covered."

"You must have a formidable faith in God, young man," says the Officer.

"Believe me, Sir, I do. I have an undying faith in Him.

"God never disappoints His children who believe in Him. We may disappoint ourselves due to our lack of patience while God takes His time to answer our prayers."

Now, during Kofi's interrogation, he says, "The victim happens to be lying dead on the corner of a dark street and I decided to help him to the nearest hospital or clinic. This is another instance for me to show that humility is alive and can be displayed."

Asked if he reported the incident to the police, Kofi says with impudence, "No, because doing so will involve long and crooked processes."

While Kofi is being grilled, Julia and Irene discuss what they should say to the police officers.

Irene says in her chat with Julia that she is the aunt of the deceased who was caught in a heated argument with another young man about a stolen goat.

Julia says she will tell the police, "After visiting his girlfriend, the victim, who is my cousin, was abducted by his rival who happened to be the ringleader of a gang of young men. It has been within the past few days that I found his dead body by the Odorkor River."

It is Julia's turn to be quizzed. "The victim is my younger brother by the name of Fearless who disappeared a few months ago but was found at a Ghanaian police station after his arrest as a suspected drug dealer," she tells the policeman.

"He is your younger brother?" Police Officer Caine asks Julia.

"Yes, Sir, Officer Caine. He is my younger brother," Julia repeats.

"Noted, miss."

"He got deported to Nigeria. A few weeks after his arrival in the country, he was run over by a speeding car that fails to stop at a traffic light where pedestrians had the green light to cross the street," Julia says as tears pour down her tender cheeks.

"Was the hit-and-run driver arrested?"

"No, Sir, Officer Caine."

"When did you hear about the accident?"

"I heard about the fatal accident on the news this morning and ran with Kofi to take him to the nearest hospital."

"I just happened to board the bone shaker as a passenger and have no knowledge of what circumstances contributed to the death of the victim," Irene told Police Officer Caine.

The two women had no idea that the interrogations were being video recorded until they saw the video. They panicked uncontrollably knowing the obvious consequences of lying to the investigator.

"You liars! You are all under arrest on suspicion of killing this teenager," Police Officer Jake pronounced, to the astonishment of Kofi who thought the officer could learn something from him for demonstrating humility to other people.

In order for the cops to take a picture of the corpse, they try to pull off the piece of cloth covering the dead body.

In the wake of doing so, an apparent cough from under the cloth spooks the policemen who experience heart attacks and fall unconscious next to the corpse.

The driver, with the help of the ladies, gently but briskly carries the police officers off the truck and places them along the roadside.

Kofi takes advantage of their incapacitation and quickly drives away to the joy of all those onboard.

Kofi drives Gold Coast Boy for about an hour and drops him off in the middle of the town where he stays overnight till, he goes back to fix his biosubmarine.

· · · · · · ● ● ● ● ◉ ● ● ● ● ● ● · · · ·

Fortunately for him, the surveillance technology in his Chimeric has been good enough to scare potential robbers, attackers, and even terrorists away as it identifies them, takes their pictures, and speaks to them when they try to touch it or are within a certain distance from it. The reconnaissance system is capable of remotely detecting destructive devices and dangerous organisms and destroying them instantaneously.

· · · · · · ● ● ● ● ◉ ● ● ● ● ● ● · · · ·

Transcontinental explorations

After struggling in Nigeria, Gold Coast Boy and two of his coworkers at IDP are awarded a two-year scholarship for advanced studies in Hyderabad, Andhra Pradesh State, India.

A send-off party is organized for the three a week prior to their departure.

In his Chimeric-79-Kano flight on a beautiful day in May, he sets sail along with Seidu and Caintor across the Atlantic Ocean from the Kano International Airport to India's Santa Cruz International Airport in Bombay with a one-week stopover in London, UK.

He is cordially welcomed to the UK as his Chimeric biosubmarine lands at the London Heathrow International Airport.

From London, they land in Bombay before finally arriving at the Namaste Training Center (NTC) at Bagunava, a village near Hyderabad. They are welcomed by the dancing water buffaloes swimming and making merry in the nearby paddy rice fields.

Four months later when the summer arrives, Gold Coast Boy and his classmates commence an eight-week educational tour of Southeastern India.

In the blazing heat of the summer, the students take the much-anticipated excursion by air. One batch flies in his Chimeric whilst the other flies in a Sajumbo jet.

Little does Gold Coast Boy know that this would mark another adventure of combing the earth with a toothpick in exploration of his lost friend's location.

By some fate, the Chimeric flight finds itself on an unknown chain of islands.

Forty-five minutes after takeoff, the giant novel transportation model is swept off by the Indian monsoon winds like a piece of leaf and could not be located on the air traffic controllers' radars. No communication could be established.

Words flying faster than the monsoons soon get to the Namaste Training Center.

In a whirl of the wind and under the instructions of the Namaste Training Center Director, Dr. Davis Dallas, a five-member Emergency Rescue Team (ERT) of three women and two men is quickly deployed under the leadership of Air Vice-Marshall Smokes to search for and rescue these passengers, who are nationals of five countries.

This sets the stage for a biorobotics revolution.

In a high technology Mutable Chameleon Helicopter (MCH) equipped with the most sophisticated advanced cameras, sound detection systems and multiple long-range ultrasensitive Radio-frequency Identification (RFID) gadgets, the resilient ERT begins its search and rescue with a mission to locate Chimeric and all nine passengers within minutes alive and well.

The camouflaged MCH biorobot, its passengers, and crew all mimic any object in any environment for safety and easy schmoozing.

All the eight trainees and Gold Coast Boy onboard Chimeric are feared dead after twenty-four hours of disappearance.

* * * * * * * ● ● ● ● ● ● ● ● ● *

Whenever the helicopter faces treacherous challenges from the wild bushfires escalated by gusty winds, undersea dangerous creatures, and dense smoke, Air Vice-Marshall Smokes becomes more defiant than ever. He even gets more determined to have a successful mission covering the marine, air and land environments.

* * * * * * * ● ● ● ● ● ● ● ● ● *

In an attempt to make an emergency landing on the unknown chain of islands, Chimeric ends up in Green Sharks Territory (GST) under the Indian Ocean.

Inhabited by free-spirited Red Hawks, the Red Hawks Islands as a nation has no military force in its own sovereignty.

The amphibious biosubmarine is spotted by the ERT fifty hours after the rescue surveillance begins.

What they see is not pleasant: an ongoing brutal battle undersea between the GST Fearsome Battalion, under the leadership of Marine Lieutenant Savagingmouth, and Chimeric where the starving green sharks are always enthusiastically happy to welcome everyone.

Air Vice-Marshall Smokes is unable to communicate with Marine Lieutenant Savagingmouth for lack of understanding of each other's languages.

He quickly posts video recordings of his ERT's discovery beneath the unknown islands on the internet to find out if anybody understands the Sharks Language (Sharklang).

Within a couple of hours, he finds Sheila Satishchandran from Sunderam City, about two hour's flight from Red Hawks Islands.

She is an internationally certified Sharklang interpreter and translator.

Being forward-looking, and for her own protection on the seas, Sheila gets certification for interpreting and translating the Red Hawks Language (Rehala).

With Sheila's Sharklang interpretation skills backed by her remote innovative teleconferencing tool, Hydrotelcomm, she informs the sharks via a mounted widescreen super ultrahigh definition television monitor on the helicopter about what brings the ERT troop undersea.

Sheila initiates a peaceful dialogue to end the undersea battle but to no avail.

In this ERT voyage, the mutable helicopter, which ploughs beneath the ocean like a fishing trawler, starts a command to mutate into a green shark. Shortly thereafter, a delay in the onset of mutagenesis gives the sharks the opportunity to launch a vicious attack on the ERT team. The hungry sharks feel their sovereignty is being invaded by some terrorists.

The presence of the mutable chameleon helicopter makes the ongoing battle against the Chimeric even more ferocious and sporadic.

An army of green sharks immediately jumps in a swoop at the Chimeric and the helicopter. There are attacks on both undersea intruders and suspected mercenaries and counterattacks.

The sharks intensify their combat on the Chimeric and the helicopter. Thousands of sharks hit both transportation systems and die like flies as their stamina wanes in the event of testing the tensile strength of the bamboo used in building Chimeric. The ocean floor is all scattered with dead sharks. The few remaining sharks surrender.

After the GST battleground regains peace, ERT is granted unconditional permission for Ibrahim's reconnaissance.

Thirty-six hours of battle lead to the rescue of Gold Coast Boy and his tour mates. The Emergency Rescue Team commander immediately orders medical evaluation of the nine passengers. Each and everyone of them is well.

"It is with great relief that we find you all safe. The Global Positioning System, or GPS, RFIDs, some Real-Time Location Systems [RTLS] and the 32D telescope in Chimeric offered big help in your surveillance," says ERT commander, Air Vice-Marshall Smokes.

"We are so overwhelmed by your rare skills. Thank you very much, Air Vice-Marshall Smokes and ERT members," Gold Coast Boy expresses his gratitude to the rescuers on behalf of his classmates, tour leader and the entire troop.

. . . .

ERT Commander Smokes and his squad send an updated report to Dr. Dallas and the Namaste Training Center staff about the finding and rescuing of the trainees. This calls for celebration with drinks of Mango Lassi, King Fisher and Hawaii Five-O.

The ERT crew is hailed as war-like heroes all over India and around the world for their discovery of Chimeric.

Following the undersea battle, the helicopter uplifts the humongous Chimeric from the undersea war zone to the Red Hawks Islands.

Can you imagine the capability of MCH?

Unimaginable.

Seeing the hawk-like Chimeric bioaircraft and the camouflaged helicopter on the islands, thousands of Red Hawks fly all over the biosubmarine and make the baobab tree which serves as the tail of Chimeric their Civic Center. The MCH which now looks like the Red Hawks, entices the islands' natives into its cabins.

The Red Hawks immediately witness PPE and bio-QnS Detective test kits floating like balloons and landing everywhere—thanks to Gold Coast Boy's foresightedness and eternal eagerness to help make the world a safer place for all human beings and animals especially at a time when every soul and creature on the planet needs to fully collaborate in curbing the spread of the pandemic IED disease.

Gold Coast Boy and Air Vice-Marshall Smokes are unable to communicate with the Red Hawks Islands' natives. Their missions are, therefore, unknown.

Three hours later, Gold Coast Boy flies his Chimeric to Sunderam City. Sheila accompanies him and his colleagues back to the islands.

As early as 5:00 a.m. local time, the Red Hawks City Hall is thronged by a multitude of Red Hawks from surrounding communities to hear Sheila.

Her arrival on the islands is marked by pomp and pageantry as it is a rare opportunity for them to hear her interpretation of the ERT and Gold Coast Boy's agenda on the islands.

A twerking dance that resonates with the sound of beads around the waists of young and old Red Hawks females can be heard beyond the precincts of the City Hall. The beads not only attract more male hawks to the site but also add a rich cultural display to the occasion. The friendly invasion of the uninvited guests in the Chimeric is a chaotic but amusing party as ERT, Gold Coast Boy and his colleagues have no choice but to quickly learn and do the red hawks dance to the admiration of the islands' inhabitants.

At the close of the dance sensation, the Mayor of Red Hawks Islands, Ms. Patience Magdalene Kwakwa,

Sheila, Gold Coast Boy, and Air Vice-Marshall Smokes take to the podium.

With Sheila's interpretation of Rehala, the Honorable Mayor welcomes the strangers and seeks to know about their mission to the islands.

Mayor Patience Magdalene Kwakwa's speeches are received by Red Hawks citizens all clad in shoe covers, face masks, gloves, light flashing disposable raincoats, and doctors' and nurses' hats that make their fashion more unique.

Sheila interprets Mayor Kwakwa's speech with a flare that is greeted with a contagious hovering round of applause by the Red Hawks Executives.

She goes on to explain how Gold Coast Boy ends up in the ocean when making an impromptu effort to land on the Red Hawks Islands.

"Honorable Mayor Patience Magdalene Kwakwa, City Executives, lovely and respectable citizens of these gorgeous islands, we are here not to invade your sovereignty, freedom and happiness. We are here, honorable citizens, to be your best friends ever on the planet.

"We are not here to defraud you. We are not terrorists. Neither are we engaged in any espionage nor underground activities.

"We are here to support your friendly and peaceful world.

"I take this privilege to inform you that a few weeks ago, Gold Coast Boy and his classmates began an educational tour of Southeastern India.

"Gold Coast Boy and his schoolmates lost contact with air traffic controllers, unfortunately.

"A super monstrous Indian monsoon off the coast of the Indian Ocean viciously swept the 4,000-kilogram (8,818-pound) Chimeric like a piece of leaf, into the bottom of the ocean, the exhausted Emergency Rescue Team discovered.

"This rare Chimeric transportation system carrying the trainees is able to withstand the savages of the monsoon; thanks to its structure built on the bamboo technology that is anticipated to protect it from treacherous weather and horrific attacks by sharks.

"His lost childhood friend, Ibrahim, is a big lover of nature and so this is a blessed opportunity to resurface in your home.

"This incident leads him to believe that you can make his dreams come true by finding his friend here," Sheila interprets Gold Coast Boy's speech.

She charms the citizens of Red Hawks Islands. She thrills the audience with her gestures and fluency in addition to the fact that the indigenes can now hear a human being speaking their own language.

"We are saddened to hear of the monsoon winds' far-reaching involvement with the Chimeric and Ibrahim's disappearances.

"On behalf of the citizens of this land, we vow every help and support for Gold Coast Boy and his friends," Mayor Kwakwa pledges to the strangers. The most spectacular and cherishable sight to write home about is, however, the gestures Sheila makes as she translates Rehala to English and vice versa.

· · · · · · · · · · ● · · · · · · · · · · ·

At the end of the celebration, Gold Coast Boy is made an honorary Deputy Mayor of the Red Hawks Islands. Sheila gets appointed as Red Hawks Roving Ambassador and Permanent Secretary. The ERT is unanimously adopted as the Islands' Military Command with Mayor Kwakwa being the Commander-in-Chief. Air Vice-Marshall Smokes becomes the top Military Advisor to Mayor Kwakwa.

Gold Coast Boy offers Honorable Mayor Patience Magdalene Kwakwa free rides on Chimeric for her annual vacations for life.

Sheila invites the twerk dancers to perform at the annual New Year's Cultural Festival in Sunderam City.

The Emergency Rescue Team appropriately names these islands, the Jubilation Islands.

Luck is not on Gold Coast Boy's side with regards to finding his lost friend. The Islands' inhabitants do not have such a visitor. They have no clues either.

One week following the ERT's arrival on the islands and all the festivities, Gold Coast Boy, his friends, Sheila and the Emergency Rescue Team depart.

· · · · · · ● ● ● ◉ ● ● ● · · · · · · ·

The students are back on the educational stream. They tour the greater number of the most fascinating places on earth that you must see at least twice in your lifetime.

"Hello ladies and gentlemen. This is Captain Gold Coast Boy speaking. On behalf of my copilot, Captain Kazara and the entire crew, I welcome you back onboard Chimeric-79A."

Taking off at exactly 07:30 hrs. and flying at an altitude of 10,000 kilometers (6,213.7 miles) above sea level the eight-week trip continues under the distinguishing comfortable identity of Chimeric flights.

But for the sprawling paddy rice fields, there is no particularly interesting scenery so the biosubmarine is high up in the sky most of the time until a brief stopover at Vijayawada, a 360-kilometer (223.6 mile) journey.

From Vijayawada, the next stop is the largest sugar factory in Asia – K.C.P. at Vuyuru where passengers engage in free conversation with the local people.

Everyone exchanges ideas on social, economic and cultural aspects of their countries of origin.

• • • • • • • • ● ● • • • • • • • • •

At exactly 07:30 hrs., Chimeric-79A takes off on a 430-kilometer (267.1 mile) flight from Vijayawada to the port city of Chennai (formerly known as Madras) and lands at the Woodland Hotel adjacent to the magnificent Savera Hotel at 18:50 hrs.

Here at the swimming pool of Woodland Hotel, Gold Coast Boy engages in casual conversations with some African students hoping that would provide a hint about his friend.

As the journey continues, Captain Gold Coast Boy slows down gracefully for passengers to see the effects of the much-publicized cyclones: houses, tents, and industries all bowed to the almighty cyclones between

Vijayawada and Chennai Demolished facilities can be seen all along the route. Dwarf and semi-dwarf crop varieties of sorghum and millet among other crops are common sights as they survived the vestiges of the vicious tropical winds that circulate counterclockwise in the northern hemisphere and clockwise in the southern hemisphere.

Some few kilometers to Chennai emerges the Bay of Bengal.

"How about having some fun watching the Indian film *Swarm*?" the tour leader asks his students as he admiringly shakes his head in a typical Indian fashion and then smiles.

"Oh yes, that's nice of you, Sir. We'll be glad to see it," the passengers readily jump at the invitation.

The next morning sees passengers onboard for a short flight to the Paddy Experiment Station on the Chennai-Arakkonam line sited at an altitude of 39.47 kilometers (24.5 miles) above mean sea level.

"There can be no better souvenir than a group photograph. So, let's all get together—our African, South American scientists and scientists of this station. Let's all get together. Cheers, everybody; cheers! and a click from Mr. Magaruchi's camera.

Part of the evening is spent at the Chennai beach and part at an "Indian music eleganza" at the Savera Hotel.

The next week sees our passengers onboard for a twelve-hour flight covering 525 kilometers (326.1 miles) to Coimbatore in the Tamil Nadu State with lodging at the teachers' hostel of the Tamil Nadu Agricultural University.

At Tamil Nadu Agricultural University, scientific agriculture as an aid to the poor farmer through a 'consultation and supply' program is at a high ebb. A series of lectures on the wide range of crops being developed and practical displays on the field and in the museum are provided.

The university tour ends with warm embraces coupled with exciting songs that magnetize many Indians to the scene.

An Indian observer makes no mistake when he says to his fellow Indian man standing next to him, "Oh, Africans are lovely people. Just see how they interact among themselves and with some few Asians and Americans in their group."

The next destination is Mysore in Karnataka State with a four-week stay in the most serene, gorgeous as well as what some travelers may describe as the most attractive city on earth, Ooty, which boasts of the most enchanting landscape you would love to capture in your memorable photo gallery.

At the outskirts of Coimbatore, a billboard blasted with pictures of lions reads, "The King of the Forest welcomes you."

This does not only tell you of the wildlife of India but also erupts the fear in the timid. The fearful side of you begins to wonder what else is there on the way. Tigers and humongous elephants?

"If it's true at all that there are lions, tigers and huge elephants on the way, then I believe they're harmless otherwise our fellow scholars on the Sajumbo Airways flight who try to scare us might not have reached Coimbatore to enjoy with us," Gold Coast Boy says to himself.

The Chimeric flight is to reach its climax in what may be classified as the 'Nilgiri Hills escapade' and whether it is the most pleasant, unpleasant or both, Ooty has the answer.

As Chimeric ascends a scarp, it meanders around it to the tune of 34 kilometers (21.1 miles) with 36 "hairpin" bends which may rather be described as "oxbow lake" or "horseshoe" bends.

Atmospheric oxygen is becoming limited as every-one's nose and ears begin to signal.

The next stopover at Ooty—the highest point on the Nilgiri Hills features a week of excursions at various sites including the Government Botanical Gardens established in 1848 which is sited at an altitude of 2,277 kilometers (1,414.9 miles) above mean sea level. The atmosphere is so misty that there are "showers" now and then.

* * * * * * * * ● ● * * * * * * * * * *

After lunch on the seventh day, a short hike to the lake crowns a relaxing moment of tours before resuming the flight at 14:10 hrs. to Mysore.

A few kilometers from Ooty is a billboard reading 2000 kilometers (1,242.7 miles) then another billboard reading 1500 kilometers (932 miles) and everyone begins to take a sigh of relief.

Proceeding with the journey a few more kilometers brings the students to sea level. "Hmmmm!" everybody takes a very deep sigh of relief immediately by laughter as passengers look at one another's faces.

"You all thought you were tough. How come there was dead silence as we were counting the 'hairpin' bends?" Falloso (from Cameroon) taunts the passengers.

"I hope you're all enjoying this flight," Nalle, a native of Thailand and one of the air hostesses enquires.

"No, I am not enjoying it in this Tamil Nadu State because there're no wines. Why at all should this State impose restrictions on alcoholic drinks? A foreigner who's allowed to take a bottle of lager beer must go through cumbersome procedures."

"Oh, it's horrible—no wines," a passenger from Brazil supports Falloso.

By 17:45 hrs., the errand finds Gold Coast Boy and his comrades in Mysore. The breeze at Krishna Raja Sagara (K.R.S. or K. R. Sagara) Lake is very captivating and everyone relaxes around the lake on which the K. R. Sagara Dam was built.

· · · · · · · · · · · ● · · · · · · · · · ·

Romance on the search trail puts the expedition in a different mode.

The exploration progresses unabated and around 09:30 hrs., Gold Coast Boy and his associates find themselves at the Central Food Technological Research

Institute (CFTRI) in Mysore where the group meets African Food Scientists from Sudan, Ghana, and Nigeria as well as other African nations.

This institute does research in several fields including food biotechnology, the canning and bottling of fruits, and the preparation of jams and fruit syrups besides fruit toffees.

Being at this renowned institute heightens Gold Coast Boy's hopes of finding his lost friend. He jumps into series of meetings with the African students and anyone he thinks may have clues about Ibrahim's whereabouts.

Gold Coast Boy spots the name tag labeled "Ama" on the multicolored T-shirt of one of the female students. He quickly runs to her.

"Hey Ama, good day. Your name suggests to me that you are from Ghana," Gold Coast Boy starts a chat with Ama who is doing her postdoctoral research work in Genetic Resources Conservation of Natural Foods.

"My name is Gold Coast Boy, and I am from Ghana myself. Em, em, sorry. I don't, I don't mean to ... excuse me with my nervousness. I don't mean to ask you a personal question, Ama."

Ama giggles and gets a kick out of Gold Coast Boy's shaky approach to her.

"What really do you have in mind, Gold Coast Boy?

"If you are thinking about asking me out on a date, think again, young man."

Ama walks away still giggling.

Running after her trying to gain courage and ask her some questions, Gold Coast Boy trips and falls flat on his face.

Ama turns around and comes to help him get back to his feet as his colleagues give the biggest tease he ever experiences in his entire life.

"Thank you so much, Ama," Gold Coast Boy expresses his gratitude to her.

"Oh, no problem. Are you okay? Now what is your problem, young man?"

"When I was a young boy in Ghana decades ago, I had a childhood friend who was deported from the country even though he was born there.

"The political environment in Ghana those days was so sickening that irresponsible and uneducated decisions made by Help Yourself politicians were rampant.

"My friend's parents were from Nigeria who had settled in Ghana for over forty years.

"The Ghana government in power those days, HY, frequently blamed the horrible economic mess of the country on foreigners. In deporting all foreigners, my friend was extradited along with his parents to Nigeria where they no longer had a home nor relatives.

"Long story short, I have been searching for my friend anywhere in the world that I find myself."

"Oh no, Gold Coast Boy. How could you be so nervous asking me if by any chance I came across this friend of yours? What is his name, anyway?"

"Ibrahim Mahamadose, also known as IBM or Ibrahim."

"What, IBM? Oh wow!

"Is he tall you think, by now? Is his skin color light complexion, does he have really dark curly hair and the body of an athlete?" Ama asks.

Her response makes Gold Coast Boy think that the search has come to an end and that Ama knows Ibrahim. He daydreams with great joy as his hands are glued onto his chest.

"Yes, oh yes! Have you seen him? Is he a student here? Ama, please, tell me. Answer me, please. Make my dreams come to an end here right now with your intervention."

"I know a guy who matches this physical description, but my memory is a little blurred about his name," she responds.

"Unfortunately, he graduated and left only one week ago. Where to, I have absolutely no idea. Maybe I can enquire from the International Students Office for you when the university is back from the long vacation in six weeks."

"Oh my God, help me Ama, please. Here is my business card with contact information. I pray you get me some good news. May God bless you."

"Thank you, Gold Coast Boy, and may God bless you too. Anyway, how long are you going to be in Mysore?"

"Just two weeks. I am on an eight-week tour with my colleagues. After our two-year training at Bagunava in Andhra Pradesh State, I will return to Africa."

"So sorry, Gold Coast Boy, I could not help you. I will have you and Ibrahim in my prayers. Stay in touch and have a safe trip back to Bagunava and Africa.

"Goodbye, Gold Coast Boy."

"Can I get a hug, Ama?"

"Sure, why not?"

Awwhhh.

What a special moment in the memory lane of combing the planet in search of a separated friend.

· · · · · · ● ● ● ● ◉ ● ● ● ● · · · · · ·

In a royal visit blended with elegant tourism, the tourists pay a courtesy call on the Maharaja (Great King) at his palace.

This is a palace adorned with all kinds of ornaments and you have to remove your shoes or sandals before entering it. As one of the most popular historical tourist centers in the world, it is a site you must visit anytime you are in Mysore.

There are still many interesting places to visit in Mysore and the Mysore Zoo is no exception.

The elephants—both Indian and African—are so gigantic that the biggest human being on earth could look like a baby worm in comparison.

Double-humped camels, rhinoceros and the omnivorous animals such as lions and tigers—you name it—are either here for amusement, to frighten the timid or both.

After the two-week stay in Mysore, the group packs bag and baggage. Off they head to Bengaluru (Bangalore), the capital city of Karnataka State. As usual, the cereal crops dominate other crops along the gently sloping land.

In Bengaluru, the group resides at Hotel Harsha while visiting the University of Agricultural Science (UAS) which researches into dryland agriculture.

The Agricultural Extension Department of UAS plays a vital role in the promotion of scientific agriculture in the State in particular and the Indian subcontinent in general by effectively linking farmers with the university.

Similarly, it aims to avoid duplication and confusion. UAS boasts of building up farmers' trust and awareness.

The group's next destination is the Scientific and Technological Museum in Bengaluru. Many have travelled by air but very few have seen that complex mechanical device of aircrafts called "the engine."

"Can you tell what the airplane's engine looks like exactly the same way as those who built it?" Gold Coast Boy ponders.

"Me and my troops can," he brags.

Talk of politics and Bengaluru will feature prominently. The giant Legislative Assembly buildings bear testimony. There are so many things to see and learn in Bengaluru.

The following day, the scholars visit the Bengaluru Botanical Gardens and the entertainment center of Majesty Cine Mall which has 46 of the 101 cinema halls. They watch a movie called *The Legal Battle: tsetse fly vs the cow.*

* * * * * * * * * ● * * * * * * * * *

Gold Coast Boy dreams on.

The entourage goes on a shopping spree after watching the movie.

During the shopping at Majesty, Gold Coast Boy sees some gifts that he thinks would be a good way of expressing his gratitude to Ama for her concerns and volunteering to fish out for him some information about Ibrahim from the International Students Office.

He ponders about what gift would be appropriate to get for her.

The phone rings. He picks up the call.

"Hello, Gold Coast Boy, how have you been all these days? This is Ama. I hope you remember me."

"My goodness!" Gold Coast Boy exclaims.

"Hey, Ama, you won't believe this. You would think I am making this up, but it is true. A second ago, I was thinking about you."

"Yeah, right, you joker. Who would fall for this, Gold Coast Boy? Not me. Haha-haa."

"Seriously, Ama, we are currently at the Majesty Shopping Center and I was wondering if you have ever been here. If not, I thought maybe, one day, we could make a quick trip here to see if we could run into Ibrahim since he is a real fashionable man. Some of our friends gave him the nickname, Dr. Fashionable."

"Haha-haa. Try something else. If I hadn't called, you would not even have remembered me, young man.

"Anyway, I just called to update you on my enquiry from the International Students Office as I had promised."

Gold Coast Boy interrupts Ama with his hopes cranking up as if he has reached the climax of his life's journey.

"Oh yes, Ama, did they tell you where he had transferred to? Did they confirm if he was a student at the Central Food Technological Research Institute?"

"Gold Coast Boy, please, take it easy and let me finish saying what I called you about."

"I sincerely apologize for cutting into your conversation so abruptly, Ama."

"For your information, the Senior Vice President of International Students Affairs tells me there is no record of any student by the name Ibrahim Mahamadose or IBM in the history of the university. Sorry for the bad news but don't give up hope. This should rather build up steam in you as you continue pursuing your dreams," Ama encourages Gold Coast Boy.

"Thank you, Ama for going all the way to the Senior Vice President on this matter. I appreciate you a lot. Thanks again. Ok, our time is up for the next phase of our excursion. Goodbye, stay blessed, and I will be in touch with you."

· · · · · · · · ● ● ● ● ● ● ● ● ● ● ● · · · · ·

On the final day in Bengaluru, just before saying *adieu* and bidding a graceful 'bye-bye', Gold Coast Boy receives yet another phone call. He answers the phone saying "Hi, my dear sweetheart Ama" thinking it was Ama. With a flattering wind of romance and surprises, Abiba says, "Excuse me, my dear Gold Coast Boy, I am not your sweetheart. This is your coordinator, Abiba, in Nigeria."

"Oooppps, sorry oooo, Abiba. I am a confused man, right now. My brains are all saturated with the thought of Ama."

"Who cares? At least, not me," Abiba frustrates him.

"Oh, okay. I hear you, Abiba. So, what is new?"

"Ibrahim has been located in the former Nigerian capital city of Lagos after prayers at the Alhaji Issah Suley Mama Mosque," she bumps up his hopes of finding Ibrahim.

Gold Coast Boy is now thrown into a dilemma. He is at a crossroads. He must decide whether to believe Abiba or not. If he chooses to listen to her, does he cut his trip to India short and return to Nigeria? Does he abandon his scholarship or take a leave of absence?

How quickly would he have to make such a decision?

After crossing his right arm on his chest as he looks up to the skies per the instructions of his father and reciting the Afadjato chant while holding the *Ahuja*, Gold Coast Boy decides to ring Ama for some consultation.

He calls her in Mysore. She is greeted with mixed feelings as to why Gold Coast Boy calls her back so soon after the end of their conversation only a few days ago.

"Is he okay? Is he missing me that much, that soon?" Ama is placed in a quagmire of despondency.

In a moment, Gold Coast Boy tells Ama about his communication with Abiba and asks for her advice on it.

As soon as his colleagues overhear him calling Ama, they start to whistle among themselves.

"Oh man, Gold Coast Boy is seriously in love with this Ama girl. He is not aware that she is a teaser just joking with him all the time. He is dreaming Ama is in love with him," Le Livre who is representing Mali ridicules him as the rest of the guys laugh and clap their hands.

Gold Coast Boy moves away from his friends to keep the conversation private.

Ama pauses for a moment and tells him to ignore Abiba. "Just don't pay attention to her, dear. She is fooling you."

"What if this is that moment, Ama?" Gold Coast Boy trembles with cold sweat for fear he may be passing up the golden light that leads him through the dark tunnel of his dream.

After a second thought, Gold Coast Boy decides to take Ama's advice and move on with his search.

"You know what, Ama? I am going to go with you on this. Thanks for being there for me, Ama. You mean so much to me."

"Thank you for listening. You are not going to regret this important decision. I wish you good luck, young man. Stay in touch."

• • • • • • • • ● ◉ ● • • • • • • • •

On this exhilarating yet challenging trip, Chimeric-79A now navigates in the land mode on the final 600 kilometers (372.8 miles) of the educational journey from Bengaluru to Hyderabad—the capital city of Andhra Pradesh State. This is a drive which, in addition to the Nilgiri Hills escapade, will go deep down in the memories of voyagers as it is expected to become the period of a genius' driving that is as skillful as anyone could witness.

But for the unequalled skills of Captain Gold Coast Boy, Chimeric-79A would have crashed, and precious African, South American and Asian blood would have been spilt in vain after a young boy freely and carelessly runs across the highway at a village around kilometer 458 (mile 284.5) on the Bengaluru-Hyderabad highway in the Madurai District.

Praises of "We thank you, God" and "Well done, Captain Gold Coast Boy," resonate almost in concert from the passengers onboard.

"Of course, it is the Omnipotent God who saved us and the little child," copilot Captain Kazara calmly says.

"Personally, from my experience as the primary pilot, navigator, owner and co-inventor of Chimeric, this is the narrowest escape I have ever been an eyewitness to.

"Life is incomplete if it goes without ups and downs, I whispered.

"Without this endurance, we would have viewed our tour from only one angle.

"Nobody prays for misfortunes in life anyway," I meditated after regaining my conscience.

As the journey moves along, policemen are observed taking measurements on the highway at kilometer 395 (mile 245.4) where two articulated trucks had collided head-on a few minutes earlier.

With these accidents, all passengers onboard Chimeric-79A get their eyes ferociously surveying the road ahead.

Gosh! There is yet another accident only 35 kilometers (21.7 miles) away from the final destination. This time, a truck is completely off the road lying on one of its sides in a valley. There is no casualty.

The tour group gets ushered into Hyderabad by 19:70 hrs. in the rains by another awful spectacle. Three huge water buffaloes are electrocuted near a cart.

Following a brief stopover at the Blue Diamond Hotel in Hyderabad for dinner at 19:40 hrs., prayers are offered to Our Lord, God, and libations are poured to honor our ancestors for bringing us back safely to Hyderabad though there are 30 kilometers (18.6 miles) more to Bagunava Namaste Training Center, the final destination.

The group safely and cheerfully lands at Bagunava at 21:14 hrs.

· · · · · · · · · ● · ● · · · · · · · · · ·

During this adrenalizing trip, Gold Coast Boy comes close to accomplishing his globe-trotting dream of finding his friend in Mysore. His interaction with Ama rekindles his hopes and perseverance.

"What did the tour offer the tourists?" one may ask.

Gold Coast Boy has some views to share: "Surely, we acquired much more knowledge in first class tourist attractions, adventure, scientific agriculture which is the only solution to the world food problem, science, and technology.

"The group also learnt firsthand the life and cultural heritage of India. On the other hand, African, Asian and Latin American cultural intelligence was highly displayed. Every member of the expeditious educational tour survived the close encounters with nature's obstacles, avoided ending the life of a poor boy, and we regained our consciousness after the descent of a steep scarp. The lions and tigers in Bengaluru scared the breath out of most people but all circumstances were handled very well.

"Coupled with what we've absorbed from the Namaste Training Center, we are going to apply under suitable conditions, all lessons learnt when we get back to our home countries," Gold Coast Boy assures the Training Department of Namaste Training Center during his graduation speech on behalf of the first-ever graduating class to be in the newly inaugurated ultramodern international training facility.

· · · · · · · ● ● ● ● ● ⬤ ● ● ● ● ● ● · · · ·

In going back to Africa at the end of the successful training and memorable tours of enchanting Indian landmarks, Gold Coast Boy returns to Nigeria with a Chimeric flight from Hyderabad to the Indian capital city of New Delhi.

The Chimeric-79B flight from New Delhi to Charles De Gaulle airport in Paris, France, makes a brief stop in the city of Tehran at dawn in the middle of tense political turmoil between the United States and Iran when some U.S. citizens are held as hostages in Tehran.

Due to the hostage situation, only the passengers terminating or connecting their flights in Tehran can disembark. What a sightseeing opportunity lost for the remaining passengers onboard.

· · · · · · · ● ● ● ● ● ⬤ ● ● ● ● ● ● · · · ·

On arriving in Paris, Gold Coast Boy is confronted by airport security officers, immigration officials and the police for several issues.

He is caught driving his Chimeric in the wrong direction when navigating his biosubmarine in the land mode. He also faces charges for his international driving license that is not recognized in France.

His fluency in French and diplomacy set him free. The magic of speaking another person's language soothes that person's heart and brings him or her closer to you.

This is exactly what happens in Gold Coast Boy's case.

The French-speaking African colleagues accompanying the English-speaking African trainees easily get to exit the airport and are permitted to roam the city until their scheduled departure from Paris.

Seeing their English-speaking African colleagues being interrogated extensively in French by the French airport officials, the Francophone African colleagues come to their aid.

Moments later, the Anglophone Africans are all permitted to tour the city of Paris.

While touring the city, Gold Coast Boy gets engaged in a casual conversation with some local French and international students from various African and Caribbean countries at the popular *J'ai faim Restaurant* near the Eiffel Tower—a famous French landmark.

As inquisitive and easy-going as he is, Gold Coast Boy gets to be the first to start the conversation. He is not intimidated by anything this time around in Paris as he was in Mysore.

He introduces himself. The students take turns to introduce themselves. The three local French students claim they lived in Nigeria for five years. Since Ibrahim moved to Nigeria, Gold Coast Boy has hopes that these French expatriates may have some knowledge about Ibrahim.

A couple of jugs of beer are shared among this new networking group prior to ordering some mouth-watering dishes from the French cuisine. Before the meals get served, two of the friends from Paris become intoxicated after drinking on empty stomachs. This leads to their long stories about how they once attended school with Ibrahim in Nigeria and that they can link Ibrahim with Gold Coast Boy in a short time.

They claim Ibrahim was in Paris on an advanced training course in mass media communication strategies.

Le Garçon Faucheux, one of the French students, tells them, "We need to come up with a roadmap." He draws an elaborate map with instructions for Gold Coast Boy to follow, leading to a specific location in Paris where his friend might be living.

"Unfortunately, my friend, I could not find Ibrahim's recent phone number. Carefully follow these directions to Studio Africa, at the corner of Rue Charles De Gaulle and L'Avenue Ton Amie. It is just a stone's throw from here. I guarantee you that Ibrahim will be sitting there, right behind a microphone," Le Garçon says as his tongue moves sluggishly around in his mouth.

Furthermore, Le Garçon the trickster quickly directs Gold Coast Boy to some news media outlets in Paris that target the African audience.

"Anything is possible. You wouldn't know until you give it a chance. If you swim and get drowned in fears to make the next move, you cannot achieve your goals," Gold Coast Boy believes.

So, he takes Le Garçon's words as true and follows those directions. Gold Coast Boy and his colleagues from the India trip take a taxi and give the driver those directions.

The female taxi driver, Mon Amie Juliette Chauffeur, knows very well there is no such location as Studio Africa. She nearly bursts into laughter when she reads the directions to the "corner of Rue Charles De Gaulle and L'Avenue Ton Amie."

For two hours, Mon Amie drives all over Paris to no avail and runs up a huge bill on the driving meter. She hands the Africans who are in Paris for the first time an exorbitant bill in Euros equivalent to US$1,100.

Tired and frustrated, Gold Coast Boy and his companions check into a hotel for another overnight stay.

The following morning, in trying to give up, Gold Coast Boy miraculously gains new energy. A new divine inspiration fills his heart, mind, and soul after reciting the Afadjato chant along with the *Ahuja* in his right hand before resuming his multicontinental odyssey.

· · · · · · · · ● ● ● ● ● ● ● · · · · · ·

From France, the African scholars head to London, UK. Gold Coast Boy is granted a four-week transit visa at Heathrow Airport. His colleagues decide to continue their journey home to Nigeria.

When Gold Coast Boy thinks it is all over—enough is enough, truly—things change for the better in London.

This is a big relief. No more misleading fraudsters at least not in London.

· · · · · · · · · · · ◉ · · · · · · · · · · ·

Ama and Gold Coast Boy continue to keep in touch from the days they got acquainted in India. Their relationship has gone from mere acquaintance to a romantic connection in which neither water nor air can pass in between them.

They got in a digital engagement over the internet while she was in India. A phone call to Ama from London the day Gold Coast Boy gets his transit visa sees Ama join him in four days. The couple continues the nearly impossible mission of probing the earth in search for Ibrahim.

Her views, faith and support, backed by her brilliance, will forever change the spectrum of his dreams.

They continue their search for Ibrahim at popular tourist hubs. The two visit Trafalgar Square where pigeons spray them with feces. Gold Coast Boy and his fiancée also visit South Kensington's Stanhope Gardens tube station where they meet a group of friends that are sincerely sympathetic and honest.

Nina Willie, the leader of this new happy-go-lucky group, loves dining and wining. She is an influential social media tycoon of the mega company *We All Multimedia* (WAM) who is well known in the UK. She creates composite images of Ibrahim from several pictures of variable ages that Gold Coast Boy has been carrying along with him and displays them on the most widely patronized social media outlets in Europe and the rest of globe.

Nina hopes someone will recognize these images and provide information about where Ibrahim might be in this world of ours which has shrunken to the size of an ant's eyeball.

"My friends, there are a few interesting concerts I would like you to check out," Nina invites them and her colleagues.

At one concert, they are entertained by melodiously singing and dancing blue dogs with the heart of a baobab tree as if each day is Christmas.

· · · · · · · · · ◉ · · · · · · · · · ·

The four weeks stay in London goes by briskly and Ama and Gold Coast Boy must depart from their friends and head to Africa. The downside of this London exploration is that Ibrahim's search and mega social media events yield no fruits.

· · · · · · · · ● ● ● ● ◉ ● ● ● ● ● · · · · ·

Gold Coast Boy hops on the next Chimeric-79C flight with Ama from London Heathrow to Kano International Airport with joy after years abroad.

At the welcome reception organized for Gold Coast Boy and his fellow trainees, Dr. S. OO gives a touching speech in which he expresses his satisfaction with the performance of his trainees during their study in India.

"Hey, Gold Coast Boy, tell us a little bit about your studies not forgetting, of course, the search for your lost friend," Dr. S. OO says with his usual gentlemanly smiles as he invites Gold Coast Boy to the stage.

There is a long-standing ovation. He is filled with mixed emotions of pure joy and a sea of plight. Gold Coast Boy starts with the joy and knowledge enrichment experienced when one travels. He enumerates all the unique events in the various places they visited in Asia.

Pointing to Ama, Gold Coast Boy says, "The highlight of it all was the unimaginable gift that God gave me and that is my fiancée, Dr. Ama Nakotey, a native of Ghana.

"I met this beautiful, brilliant biotechnology genius at the Central Food Technological Research Institute in Mysore."

Ama is welcomed with great joy and everyone is so happy for Gold Coast Boy for the precious God-given gift.

"The saddest experience from the journey was my failure in accomplishing my dream of seeing my childhood friend again. The combing got entangled in several webs, wedges and near disasters. Luckily, though, Ama had joined me in scrutinizing all efforts to find my friend," Gold Coast Boy gets on with his speech in a recollection of agonizing memories.

* * * * * * * * * ● ● ● ● ● ● ● ● ● * *

After a brief stay in Nigeria, Gold Coast Boy takes a trip to his native Ghana to bid farewell to his family and friends prior to leaving for further studies in America.

Gold Coast Boy comes back with a future wife who is a proud daughter of motherland Ghana.

He is happy to see his parents still alive but bogged down by the onset of old age.

A sentimental melodrama springs up among his siblings and friends. He is excited to see old friends and the extended family members as well.

Before Gold Coast Boy gets the chance to introduce Ama, Teye, as usual, quickly jabs his brother. "Good to see you back not marrying a lady from 'outside'. You would have subjected mom to a marvelously complicated heart attack in a flash.

"You already know women from outside our country, tribes and culture normally don't fit in. They don't wake up at dawn to sweep the compound and they can't carry on their heads the earthenware water pot when they walk one mile to the nearest water well to fetch water.

"Worst of all, they cannot cook a sumptuous meal of water yam, cocoyam and plantain *fufu*," Teye infuriates everyone.

Mercy immediately knocks some sense into Teye's head in anguish. "You need to be in the neuropathology doctor's office for a thorough evaluation. First of all, women from outside can do everything your local tribeswomen can do. You just can't get up and make these discriminatory claims. Secondly, Gold Coast Boy hasn't even had the opportunity to introduce his guest. Who tells you they are married, notorious intruder Teye?"

· · · · · · · · · · ● ● · · · · · · · · · · ·

Gold Coast Boy continues his ceremonial occasion after that distraction. "Well, well, well, my main man Dad, who is also my best friend, lovely mom, ladies, and gentlemen, I am so, so happy to introduce to you my loving, caring and sweet fiancée whom I met in India, Dr. Ama Nakotey," Gold Coast Boy says, highly elated.

The Ghanaian traditional wedding engagement and the much-anticipated wedding take place two days later.

Nobody could skip the colorful traditional wedding engagement, which normally draws a crowd of five hundred family and clan members, extended relatives, friends and the general community most of whom are self-invited.

Gold Coast Boy and Ama get married at the Asesewa Presbyterian Church and have the wedding reception at the Asesewa Biotechnology Center of Excellence.

Oleman walks to the stage and makes a short statement.

"On behalf of the family, clan, and all well-wishers, I am highly ecstatic to welcome Dr. Ama Nakotey to the family. We are all proud of you two. May you both continue to support each other with love as strong as the bamboo tree.

"Safe journey to America and always keep us in your prayers as we also keep you in our hearts, souls, minds and prayers. Come back to visit us before we depart to heaven. Stay protected and blessed."

Ama's father, Dr. Evans Narh Sackitey Nakotey, takes a turn to bless the newlyweds. In his speech, he traces the baby steps of his only daughter all the way to the giant leaps she has made throughout her life since the sixth grade when she began winning various athletic and academic honors.

"Ama was the recipient of the highly contested Debating Society Champion-of-the-Year Award at the Akosombo International Experimental School. In her senior year, Ama was elected the President of the Student Governance Body (SGB) and became the first-ever female in the school's forty years' history to hold that post which was dominated by males," Dr. Nakotey recollects.

Without saying too much and boring the audience with what some people may consider as superstition, Dr. Nakotey adds, "She made her family proud. Above all, she has made all girls even prouder.

"We love you and pray for your continued success and happiness in your marriage, our pumpkin pie."

Ama's mother, Dr. (Mrs.) Beatrice M. Nakotey wishes the new couple well in their mission and vision in life. She presses on to say that they should leave no stone unturned in fulfilling God's promise of 'be fruitful and multiply' in their youthful ages.

"Give us five girls and two boys—our seven grand-children," she says as she raises her seven fingers to the heavens.

Mrs. Oleman expresses some concerns before saying the closing prayer.

"My son and daughter-in-law, as your global combing trip heads to the U.S., there is a major concern I have.

"It is particularly about your and Ama's safety and dignity in the U.S. or in any country you find yourselves in.

"Do not indulge in unnecessary arguments or debates be they political, professional or personal. Do not hang out with gangs. Always carry your Bible with you and remember where you come from. Hold high your dignities and those of the Oleman and Nakotey families.

"You may not come back to meet us—your old folks Oleman, me, and Dr. and Dr. (Mrs.) Nakotey. Keep us in your daily prayers as we keep you in ours every day."

Mrs. Oleman offers a prayer and brings the occasion to a happy ending.

"May the Lord bless you, keep you and your children safe, guide you all the days, nights and in between for the rest of your lives. To you, my daughter-in-law and my

son, I wish you a happy and solid marriage with the longevity of the baobab tree. Amen."

The crowd applauds in the midst of resonating
sounds of "Amen."

* * * * * * * * * * ⚫ * * * * * * * * * *

Ama and Gold Coast Boy take to the skies on their
way to America via his duty station in Nigeria.

The route takes them to New York City, the U.S. side
of Niagara Falls in the State of New York, the Mall of
America in Minnesota, and the Liberty Bell in the *City of
Brotherly Love*—Philadelphia—in the Commonwealth of
Pennsylvania.

Other sites on this hunt stream include Greyhound
Bus stations along the Tennessee Valley. Additional loca-
tions comprise the Florida Keys, the Grand Canyon in the
State of Arizona, the State of Georgia, the corn fields of
Iowa, the annual Drake Relays athletics events in Des
Moines, Iowa, and the Hoover Dam also in the State of
Arizona.

His flight, Chimeric-79-USA, takes off from Kano
International Airport. On arrival at New York City's John F.
Kennedy (JFK) International Airport, Gold Coast Boy and
Ama are met by anti-GMO demonstrators from the group

No Messing Up with God's Creations (NOMUGC). The demonstrators accuse them of attempting to destroy and destroying the environment while messing up with God's creations.

No amount of scientific, religious or diplomatic arrangement of words or phrases is acceptable for NOMUGC. The demonstrators insist the couple should be jailed.

However, there is no law in America, apparently, saying that genetic engineers or biotechnology professionals are criminals when they create products or services to help humanity, especially when the benefits outweigh the risks.

Both are let off the hook.

· · · · · · · · ● · · · · · · · · · ·

In the land-navigation mode, Chimeric hits the road to the New York side of Niagara Falls where they are stared at by many onlookers and children who think they are seeing an outer space vehicle. In a fast-food restaurant, the couple socializes with tourists from around the world.

Following a series of conversations, Gold Coast Boy asks some of the people he chats with, "Would it be prudent spending years searching for a lost friend?"

"As a matter of fact, I am in the middle of doing so as we speak," twenty-three-year-old Brittney responds amazed at herself noticing that someone else is putting on the same shoes.

"I lost touch with my friend Joyce right after high school graduation."

Visibly moved, Brittney says, "Some of my friends led me to believe that Joyce had moved, was married, and had changed her legal name and phone number."

As Gold Coast Boy begins to recapitulate his experiences, Ama takes down notes to formulate strategic maneuvers in their future episodes.

The trip to Niagara Falls ends with no ceremonial events.

* * * * * * * * * ● ◉ ● ● ● ● ● * * * *

Arriving in Minnesota, Gold Coast Boy sees some white flurries falling from the sky. He becomes curious and opens his palms out to catch them. As the weather is above freezing temperature, the snow flurries melt right away in his palms. Next, he touches his head to find out if the flurries are stuck in his hair. No, they vanish quickly like magic.

"What trick is this white sand playing on me?" he asks with a mixture of smile and puzzle.

Ama is surprised by his observation and reaction.

"These are snow flurries, young man, not white sand," she whispers to hide her embarrassment.

"You mean this is the first time in your life you are seeing snow?"

"Believe it or not, yes, this is the first time I am seeing snow."

Ama giggles a little bit and says, "You ain't seen snow yet. You wait till we get to northern Minnesota and you will see what snow is and what it can do to you. Better dress up warmly, dear."

The following day, Ama and her husband rent a car from the Minneapolis suburb of Eden Prairie to go to Duluth, Minnesota, a city well-known for its long, cold winters. Gold Coast Boy ignores Ama, taking her advice as a joke, and dresses in a spring jacket and baseball hat. Ama jokes hilariously, "You are a sandwich short of a picnic, I think!"

The weather is sunny and bright with beautiful blue skies. The strong winds make the temperature feel like -20 degrees Fahrenheit (-28.9 degrees Celsius).

The rental car they ride in skids off the road into a ditch due to a stretch of an icy patch. The Minnesota State Trooper patrolling the area to get motorists off the highway shows up at the scene.

In a short conversation with the State Trooper in the freezing temperatures, water dripping from Gold Coast Boy's eyes turns into icicles that get his eyes "glued." Temperatures are so cold that the heat in the car does not work.

A blast from the hood of the car ignites a fire. Within the twinkle of an icicled eye, there is a huge assembly of several fire trucks, ambulances, police cars, and terrorism-detection security personnel.

Paramedic officials rush Gold Coast Boy to the nearest hospital for treatment of multiple health injuries and gets discharged after two days in the Duluth Methodist Hospital.

Ama who is dressed appropriately for the weather suffers no ill health.

"We sometimes take the police as our rivals due to some crimes some of them commit against some people; in particular people of color and especially unarmed black men. This is one of the moments you have demonstrated that the police are capable of performing their noble duties with trust and nonviolence whilst faithfully protecting themselves from harm and danger.

"You have become our friends. I sincerely express my profound appreciation to you all and pray that all policemen and policewomen in the Minneapolis-St. Paul Twin Cities metropolis in Minnesota—and in America for that matter—and around the world learn from you," Ama tells the police officers honestly, from her heart, emphasizing the fact that police brutality and brutality in homes, schools, sports, entertainment, the animal kingdom or any source have no place in modern civilization.

Freedom and Justice rules supremely as transcribed and enshrined in Ghana's *Coat of Arms* which was authoritatively crafted with passion and patriotism by one of the world's most creative and innovative artists, Nii Amon Kotei.

From Duluth, they return to Eden Prairie before heading to Bloomington, a suburb of Minneapolis, in the Chimeric.

At the largest shopping mall in the United States— the Mall of America—located in Bloomington, Ama and Gold Coast Boy choose to take some time off to relax from their stressful exploration.

"How about hopping on this humongous roller coaster ride in this mall rather than shopping?

"After all, our travels so far have been filled with roller coaster emotions," Gold Coast Boy tries to persuade Ama.

"Oh, no problem. No problem at all as long as you can hold on to me so that I don't fall, my bamboo man."

They purchase tickets for the ride and queue in a long line they have never seen anywhere on their trips.

As they enjoy the ride, Gold Coast Boy keeps taking a glance at a fellow black man who resembles his friend. He is so focused on this Ibrahim look-alike gentleman that he falls from the roller coaster. He gets injured and is rushed to the Bloomington Hospital.

His x-rays and other tests show that his condition is not life-threatening.

"Let's get out of this State, Ama. It is no fun out here. Considering the icicled eyes and injury during the roller coaster ride besides our inability to find Ibrahim here, I would say let's get out of here in no time," he says upon his discharge from the hospital.

· · · · · · · · · · ● ● ● ● · · · · · · · · · · ·

The couple travels to the Commonwealth of Pennsylvania.

Being in America for a while now, Ama and Gold Coast Boy decide to make Philadelphia their new home.

Ama gets the chance to do a second postdoctoral research at the University of Pennsylvania Human Genomics Innovation Center (HGIC) in Philadelphia.

Gold Coast Boy is offered a senior biotechnology research scientist position in Exton, Pennsylvania, with Biotechnology Evolving Innovations (BEI), a start-up bio-pharmaceutical company.

· · · · · · · · · ● · · · · · · · · · ·

A number of years after settling in Pennsylvania, Ama is invited to an international biotechnology confer-ence at Victoria Falls in Zimbabwe.

The conference theme is "Keep the momentum going: We still have a long way to go."

Gold Coast Boy takes a vacation and goes with Ama to Victoria Falls, the venue for another event, the *Search And Find* (SAF) Concert.

On one beautiful Friday afternoon in September when the couple begins preparing to pack and head to the Victoria Falls conference, Gold Coast Boy gets a phone call from London, UK.

"*Krring, krrring.* The phone rings.

Gold Coast Boy picks up the phone.

"Hey, Gold Coast Boy, this is Nina from the UK. What are you doing exactly two fortnights from this weekend?" Nina asks.

"Hey, Nina, what are *you* doing exactly two fortnights from this weekend?" Gold Coast Boy counter quizzes Nina by resonating her question.

"I am covering an event in Victoria Falls in the African country of Zimbabwe that week for my Company, WAM," Nina answers.

"Holly, teeny, teeny, tiny world. My wife and I are going to be in Victoria Falls that weekend too! He exclaims with excitement.

* * * * * * * * * * ● ○ ○ ● * * * * * * * * *

Two weeks later, Ama and Gold Coast Boy board Chimeric-79-VF flight from Philadelphia International Airport to Victoria Falls, with stops at New York's JFK International Airport, London Heathrow International Airport, Johannesburg's O.R. Tambo International Airport, and Harare International Airport.

Nina joins them at Heathrow. This calls for a happy reunion of the trio in London. As usual, Nina is the first to pop open the wine and champagne bottles.

Nina starts a conversation. "So, what's going on in Victoria Falls, guys, if I may ask? Have you found Ibrahim there?" Nina further seeks to rejuvenate chatting from the last meeting of the three in London.

"Oh, I hope we find him there. As a matter of fact, Ama has been invited by the International Society of Contemporary Biosciences to make an oral presentation and I am joining her on the trip. I will, of course, use this occasion to campaign for his search.

"By the way, what event are you covering?"

"I am one of the co-hosts of *Search And Find [SAF]*, an international fundraising concert aimed at raising US$5 million to help efforts in finding and rescuing people who are missing or abducted.

"I am wondering if you would be interested in joining us as one of the session keynote speakers, Gold Coast Boy."

"Absolutely. Why not? I will be more than happy to join your noble cause, Nina."

"Your story about Ibrahim really touched the nerves of my heart in London years ago and it still does."

"You have such a kind heart, Nina. It is fantastic you still remember my lost friend."

"I am sure there are several people around the world in the same boat as you, searching for someone like Ibrahim and we can touch their hearts too," Nina says as she wipes tears running down her cheeks like the water falling off the Victoria Falls.

She goes on to describe what motivated her to partner with SAF.

* * * * * * * * ● ⊛ ● ● ● ● ● * * * * *

Children and Youth Displays (CYD), an educational and entertainment (edutainment) roving ambassadors' group, takes the stage immediately before the start of the US$5 million SAF Concert. Nina promptly introduces Gold Coast Boy to the co-hosts and the audience.

Shortly thereafter and to everyone's astonishment, the Victoria Falls SAF Concert pavilion gets bombarded with colorful PPE and bioQnS Detective test kits dropping from his Chimeric-like parachutes. Gold Coast Boy donates these items to help curtail the spread of the IED disease.

What a pleasant, safe, and peaceful environment it is to see all the children and the entire audience wearing PPE and medical professionals among them fully prepared to use the bioQnS Detective whether or not any person complains of possible IED symptoms.

In his captivating speech titled "One Small World: Nobody Can Hide or Be Hidden," Gold Coast Boy pays tribute to all the children, young men and women who vanished into unknown environments during the past four decades under numerous circumstances and hopes they get found and rescued safely.

Oh, not forgetting his friend, he makes a heartfelt appeal to reunite with Ibrahim alive and safe.

* * * * * * * * * ✹ * * * * * * * * * * *

The aim of CYD is to direct global attention to the talents children have and how they could use such talents to make the world a better place to live in for generations to come.

In the 6 to 9 years age group named the Early Innovators, Liam Spencer from Stanhope Gardens Municipality in London, UK, is phenomenal with his voice as he sings his internationally popular *Kip-movin* song.

Among children in the 10 to 13 years group (Curious) is Nene Phronesis of Tema Harbor City in Ghana. Riding a wheeled-boat in a float during the concert, Nene keeps the audience on its feet for hours as he charms everyone with his unparalleled magnificent saxophone performance that Adolphe Sax, the Belgian who invented the saxophone, would have been proud of.

In the other sensational age group comprising 14 to 19 year-olds (Influencers), Sangeeta Shukriyaa of New Delhi, India, steals the show with her spectacular cinematic exhibition of ingenious Indian artistry.

From Pittsburgh, Pennsylvania in the U.S comes the highly esteemed orator Lisa Lakisharp in the 20 to 29 years age group (Confidence) who makes a vibrant speech calling all leaders around the planet to be fully engaged in ensuring the safety and protection of humankind.

The weeklong concert raises US$10 million.

· · · · · ● ● ● ● ● ◉ ● ● ● ● ● ● · · ·

On the last day of the SAF event, there is a standing ovation the entire time as the audience dances to the "Tena, tena, tenacious" lyrics of Jos and Oaks (known for short as J & O), the celebrated edutainment legends on the continent of Africa, and shakes Victoria Falls to the extent that the usual loud noise of the water running down the falls gets drowned out even from miles away.

Nina gives thanks to all participants and sponsors at the end of the event. She calls for the unconditional love, cherishing and caring for one another in every community around the world. She also guarantees all and sundry that the US$10 million would be used with stringent accountability to help in the search and rescue of missing and abducted people around the world.

Additionally, Nina encourages Capacity and Human Resources Development programs to heighten aware-ness about vigilance and safety.

Three days after Victoria Falls, Nina, Gold Coast Boy and Ama fly back to London, UK, where Nina disem-barks the Chimeric-79-PA flight. The couple continues to Philadelphia, Pennsylvania.

· · · · · · · · · ● ● ● · · · · · · · · ·

Back in the Philadelphia metropolitan area, they head on from Exton, a rapidly booming biotechnology hub in West Chester County to the Liberty Bell two weeks after their arrival from Victoria Fallfs. Propelling in the air-navigation mode of Chimeric, they land on the ocean nearest to the Liberty Bell, one of the most famous American historic landmarks.

Unfortunately, all strategic partnerships to locate Ibrahim at this popular global tourist attraction center prove futile.

· · · · · · · · · ● ● ● · · · · · · · · ·

Gold Coast Boy gets invited to a wedding ceremony to be officiated by his long-time friend, Pastor Alex. The ceremony is scheduled to take place at the LubuKoyine Global Salvation Church in Tanzania.

At the recommendation of Pastor Alex to the wedding planning committee, Gold Coast Boy gets appointed to be the Master of Ceremonies (MC) at the wedding reception.

Nine months after returning from Victoria Falls, Gold Coast Boy and Ama board Chimeric-79-SKR to SokoRubinda Christian Seminary where they are hosted by Pastor Alex and Nancy.

Taking a break from Chimeric, Gold Coast Boy decides to take Pastor Alex up on his offer to drive them on the two-hour journey from the SokoRubinda to the LubuKoyine Global Salvation Church which is located a few meters (yards) below the heels of the opulent scenery of Mountain Kilimanjaro in the eastern African nation of Tanzania.

Little do Pastor Alex and his entourage know they will be experiencing an eye-popping miracle in a car's trunk.

Going to the wedding at LubuKoyine, the rainbow-colored Nissan Datsun salon car driven by the pastor is hijacked by armed robbers who have formidable ties with the local police. Gang leader Abimelech Yirenchest is a notorious rapist, drug dealer, idolater and juju man who boasts he will never be captured.

The passengers in the car, Nancy, Ama and Gold Coast Boy panic as they struggle to locate their cell phones to make that frantic call to the police.

Poor you, people.

Little do they know the robbers have strong business relations with the police.

In the town of Kitan, on the way to the wedding, the armed robbers notice a man who withdraws some money from the ATM (automatic teller machine) near a convenience store.

Of late, armed robbery, rape, abduction and other forms of violence have been on the rise in this town.

The armed robbers trail the rainbow car.

When the car gets to a remote forested area, Abimelech, the driver of the four-gang members who have no face masks and do not disguise themselves, drives the van extremely close to the pastor's car. He provokes him by nearly hitting his vehicle.

Abimelech overtakes him and parks the steel-plated Toyota Rover 1 van across the street to block him. Pastor Alex nearly hits the van. The pastor stops immediately and attempts to reverse his Datsun so he can drive away in the opposite direction but there is no time to do that as Abimelech and one of his accomplices get out of the van right away and point their guns at the pastor who is commanded to get out of his car without delay.

He does.

Abimelech, in an effort to take over the pastor's seat, forces the car door to open while pointing his gun at the unarmed pastor. He orders Pastor Alex out of his car. When forcibly opening the car's trunk to compel Pastor Alex to hide in there, Abimelech finds to his dismay Nancy already hiding in there.

She panics and screams.

"Huh, what are you doing in here?" Abimelech asks. He gets aggravated and is subjected to a high-magnitude shock wave.

"You must be loaded with lots of money. That can be the only reason you chose not to sit in the car with your friends," he says furiously.

Nancy is promptly ordered to get out of the trunk and hand over all the money she has as the gun is pointed at her nose.

She complies in haste.

Nancy is forced back into the trunk.

Pastor Alex is ordered to surrender all the money he has on him. He complies and gets squeezed in there with her.

In the front passenger seat of the Datsun sits Gold Coast Boy trembling with fear as he quietly recites his Afadjato chant. He quickly attempts to hide his body under the front passenger seat so that nobody can see him, he thinks.

Ama, sitting in the back seat holds her palms over her face and praying for God's salvation. The second armed robber sits in the back seat with Ama.

The remaining two armed robbers in the Toyota Rover 1 follow the Nissan Datsun car now driven by Abimelech very closely.

After driving for an hour, the robbers stop at a deserted parking lot along the road.

The pastor and Nancy are let out of the car trunk.

The armed robbers ask all the victims of this car-jacking to vanish immediately with the warning from Abimelech Yirenchest: "You know us and can see that we have not disguised ourselves. You can see our faces and recognize us. Similarly, we can recognize you all.

"You must keep your mouths shut and not tell anybody about us or what you have gone through. If you do, you will be killed," he threatens, and the four robbers disappear.

Pastor Alex takes over his car and speeds like a drunken tiger that has lost its sense of direction.

As a matter of fact, the pastor is lost as he does not know where he is now.

The stranded travelers are now between a rock and a hard place: driving back the wrong way to a location they know and lodging a complaint at the nearest police station.

The freed hostages ask for directions from where they got dumped at to LubuKoyine village.

Pastor Alex is told to turn around and drive in the opposite direction. Afraid of running into the gang of robbers again, he refuses to follow the direction.

The pastor and his friends decide to defy the threat of the armed robbers as they take solace from their divine beliefs. They choose to file a report at the nearest police station forty-five minutes' drive down the road.

At the counter, Pastor Alex, Gold Coast Boy and the two beautiful young ladies are asked by the supervising police officer on duty to take a seat in the conference room. He says he will be attending to them shortly.

They sit for ninety minutes with nobody attending to their case. Not knowing that the police officers are shareholders of the operations of the gang members, they sit comfortably and patiently waiting for justice and protection that do not exist.

The period of ninety minutes happens to move ninety times slower than the pace of a drunken turtle. Tired of waiting and feeling neglected by law enforcement officers who are supposed to protect them, they decide to leave the police station.

They are shown the exit with no questions asked, and they head back in the direction they had come from. With God on their side, they end up at LubuKoyine the next morning.

Pastor Alex and his entourage are greeted by the huge audience that wondered if they had changed their minds about attending the wedding.

The marriage of Mr. Francis Lubinza-Mpenzi and Ms. Francisca Nakupenda Mponzi takes place at the LubuKoyine Global Salvation Church the second day after the armed robbers' attack.

The pastor vividly narrates the car trunk miracle they experienced on their way to the wedding ceremony. The congregation joins them in a short devotion to cherish the Lord for the guidance on their journey through the dark tunnels. Everyone sees this miracle as a testimony of God's unfailing protection.

Wasting no time, Pastor Alex goes, "And now, for the reason we are all assembled here today. We are all gathered here to witness and celebrate the union of our lovely friends, Francis and Francisca, who from today till the end of life are called Mr. and Mrs. Lubinza-Mpenzi."

After leading them to exchange the marriage vows, Pastor Alex declares them as legally married husband and wife.

An hour later, the wedding reception takes place at the Traveler J's Hotel about five minutes' drive from the church.

Taking the stage, Gold Coast Boy welcomes the crowd in French, which is the language of the newlywed and the Francophone audience in the LubuKoyine community where English and French are the official languages.

He also expresses his appreciation for the invitation in addition to his appointment to host the memorable romantic occasion.

He is given a standing ovation as he speaks their language and momentarily steals the attention from the just-married couple.

"*Attention s'il vous plaît, belles personnes. Aujourd'hui est un jour mémorable et joyeux pour les nouveaux mariés, M. et Mme Lubinza-Mpenzi.*" ["Attention please, beautiful people. Today is a memorable and joyful day for the new-lyweds, Mr. and Mrs. Lubinza-Mpenzi."].

"Today is also a happy day and a sad day," he announces.

"We don't want to hear about the sad one!!," a young lady in the audience shouts.

"Let's hear the good news first!!," another person screams.

Pretending not to hear these distractions, Gold Coast Boy goes on to take this opportunity to announce his search and hopes of finding the long-lost friend, Ibrahim.

Gold Coast Boy briefly recounts the circumstances leading to the separation between him and his child-hood friend. He clearly paints the picture of the subse-quent voyages he has been making to find Ibrahim.

"So, please, join me in combing the planet for my lost friend," he pleads.

The audience sympathizes with him. It also pledges to help in the search for Ibrahim.

A hotel manager on duty watching the news on a TV in the hotel lobby informs the wedding guests through an intercom of a breaking news alert in the middle of Gold Coast Boy's wedding reception speech.

The public broadcast announcement on the Kigali-based Underground Fiber Optic Cable Broadcasting Network (UFOCBN) breaking news syndicate abruptly halts the event temporarily. The news is also heard on a radio in the wedding reception area.

"Abimelech Yirenchest, the ring leader of the four-member armed robbery gang, has been captured at the Kigali International Airport by the International Police Squadron headquartered in Kigali, Rwanda, as he tried to board a flight back to the port city of Dar es Salaam in Tanzania following a long hide out in Rwanda," it is reported.

"The gang made up of three men and one woman, who are usually undisguised, has formed a coalition with the Kitan local police in causing horrific panic in Tanzania. Following an existing agreement between Tanzania and Rwanda, plans are underway to extradite him to his native country, Tanzania," the report continues.

"A civilian-military tribunal has been set up to investigate the motivation and criminal activities of all parties involved. Anyone found guilty of an offence will be guaranteed life imprisonment."

The audience stands up, claps, and cheers crazily in appreciation of the UFOCBN breaking news.

Perplexed for a moment, Gold Coast Boy continues his speech. "Now we can sleep peacefully. Where was I? Help me out, lovely people."

He ushers in the couple, who waves to the huge crowd.

"Let us enjoy to the fullest with Mr. and Mrs. Lubinza-Mpenzi! Let's hear the sounds of the calabash drums! Let's dance the dance of the people and toast with the freshly brewed palm wine, red and white wines, *akpeteshie*, whisky and soda to the merriment of the newlyweds!" Gold Coast Boy enchants the audience.

The ceremony ends with a vibrant cultural display reminiscent of the ancestors who ensure a happy, prosperous, and healthy marriage longer than the lives of Methuselah and the African baobab tree combined.

The news broadcast not only supports Gold Coast Boy's SAF Concert theme in Victoria Falls— "One Small World: Nobody Can Hide or Be Hidden"—but also relieves the people of Kitan.

Seven days following the UFOCBN News report, the undisguised gang and its associates are put on trial. Those found guilty are sentenced to life imprisonment.

Three days after the wedding, Gold Coast Boy and Ama head back to the United States on the hunt trail.

* * * * * * * * ⬤ * * * * * * * * *

When combing the earth continues in America, an online advertisement in the *Baltimore Rainbow Newspaper* directs Gold Coast Boy's navigation compass to head to the Baltimore Inner Harbor in the State of Maryland.

The advertisement highlights Alhaji Inusa Mama Sule as one of the session keynote speakers at the semi-annual Baltimore Inner Harbor Literary Get Together themed *"Next Generation Literature (NextGen Literature): Where Do We Go From Here?"*

Alhaji Inusa is featured to share his views on "The Impact of Social Media on Digital Literature in Education Globally."

He confidently argues that although social media (s.m.) can be a powerful means for substantiating DNA testing evidence assuming ethical and legal principles apply, some of its outlets have the potential to damage literature worldwide if it is not rigorously regulated.

Among other predicaments, "Students at all rungs of the educational ladder who get addicted to s.m. platforms are no longer able to spell words correctly, nor can they differentiate between *hear* and *here,* for instance, or write sentences that are grammatically correct. Ask them to identify idioms, prepositions, and metaphors in sentences. That becomes a major problem," he alleges.

For these concerns, Alhaji Inusa calls for high profile educationists, regulators, technologists, policy makers and other experts to take immediate action to rectify the situation before it becomes an educational pandemic.

It is imperative, however, to point out that social media alone cannot be blamed for educational deterioration and digital literature degradation. High quality teachers, family, friends, social upbringing and peer pressure, for instance, can significantly impact education globally.

Education is losing its luster because most of the youth don't make genuine efforts to read. Quality education begins with reading and reading nourishes the mind, soul, society and the future.

* * * * * * * * * * ● * * * * * * * * * * *

Two things really piqued Gold Coast Boy's interest in this event. One is that Alhaji Inusa Mama Sule is the name of Ibrahim's younger brother. The other is Ibrahim's love of English Literature for which he collected the Best Literature Student prize in his class during Annual Speech and Prize-Giving Day Ceremonies at Ghana National College in Cape Coast, Ghana.

"If Ibrahim's younger brother is a keynote speaker at this event, you can bet Ibrahim is going to be there, I guarantee you, Ama," Gold Coast Boy assures his wife.

"Just be careful, my dear. Don't run before you can walk. Don't get overly optimistic. You have been burnt many times in the past by false leads."

"Many times, I have been burnt. Many times, I have been revived to pursue my dreams.

"We shall navigate Chimeric to the Baltimore Inner Harbor and find Ibrahim there, Ama."

"I wouldn't go down that road if I were you. If you say so, let's go!" Ama gives in.

Off they go.

"Ibrahim, here we come. We shall find you. Baltimore Inner Harbor, here we come. Make our dreams come unfolded," Gold Coast Boy says self-assuredly whilst beseeching at the same time.

"Does this gentleman really look like Ibrahim?" Ama whispers to Gold Coast Boy after the speaker was introduced to the attendees.

"I strongly believe so, Ama."

"What makes you so poised, my man?"

"His light skin complexion, crooked nose, broad front teeth, dense eye brows, ear lobes that stick out at a 90-degree angle and his distinctive Nigerian accent."

The pair gets to have a one-on-one chat with Alhaji Inusa after his speech. Following a series of probes as to whether Alhaji Inusa once lived in Ghana, Gold Coast Boy gets disappointed to learn that Alhaji Inusa never set foot on Ghanaian soil.

"I am a 100 percent Nigerian breed, educated in Nigeria and worked in Nigeria. I don't have and never had relatives in Ghana," Alhaji Inusa sinks Gold Coast Boy's hopes of finding Ibrahim at the Baltimore Inner Harbor Literary Get Together.

With a broken heart and tears almost soaking his shirt, Gold Coast Boy and Ama depart from Maryland and head to Tennessee.

* * * * * * * * * ● ● ● * * * * * * * *

At a Greyhound bus station in the Tennessee Valley, Tennessee, they both join a casual soccer game after Ama politely asks if they could join in for a few minutes.

"Hey guys, we are going to thrill you with real fancy football moves," Gold Coast Boy tells the players after they were granted permission by one of the captains to play.

"Hello mister, this is not football. It is soccer," a team member responds with laughter.

"In Africa, soccer is popularly called football," Gold Coast Boy fires back.

Most immigrants from the soccer world get confused when they get to America where American football is more popular than soccer.

A teenage boy looks at Ama and says, "You want to play with us? Girls don't play football here. It is a boys' game, miss."

Ama puts both hands on her waist and looks at the boy in a funny way. She dribbles the soccer ball around the boy who sees the dribble of his lifetime. He has never seen a girl play soccer with such titanic skills.

"That is enough for you, boy. Next time, you don't dream of challenging a girl when it comes to playing football.

"Get it?"

"Yes, I get it, Miss."

While Ama and Gold Coast Boy impress the youth soccer teams in Tennessee, Nina calls Gold Coast Boy from London, saying that a subscriber to one of her channels tells her a story that she conceives holds water. In the story, the subscriber convinces her that Ibrahim is in the Florida Keys.

This immediately prompts the couple to navigate the Chimeric biosubmarine in the air mode and fly to Florida.

The two defy the potential life-threatening warnings of hurricane Chiminski that has been ploughing the Florida Keys, which frequently get hit by highly destructive rainstorms.

As they approach the Miami International Airport in Florida, Chimeric is put to the test. On its descent, the biosubmarine, with its long tail of baobab tree, is swept swiftly like a light kite in flight at night onto the bright surface of the Atlantic Ocean by hurricane Chiminski.

"Wow, nature can be mean and powerful, but God is the most powerful," Ama says with unfailing faith.

After some prayers and the *Ahuja-Afadjato* chanting by Ama and Gold Coast Boy, Chimeric begins navigation in the marine mode that takes them to the bottom of the Atlantic Ocean for a whole week without any damage or injury to its occupants.

The rampant Chiminski massacre in the Florida Keys takes many lives and causes millions of dollars of property damage as its anger is watched live and shared all over the world.

Gold Coast Boy contacts Nina in London and his parents in Ghana to assure them that God is in control.

A similar assurance is transmitted to Ama's relatives who are also in Ghana.

When the Chiminski torture calms down, the couple envisions it as an omen of brilliant lights leading them into the future of their cruise and they surface onto the land with revitalized confidence.

The emotions at the Florida Keys are so heartbreaking that talking about the search for a lost childhood friend would not get into anybody's ears or gain any amount of sympathy, they think.

Ama and Gold Coast Boy rather end up joining several rescue efforts to bring back sanity to the families of thousands of perished lives and survivors including children. In addition, they donate US$10,000 to help in recovery missions.

* * * * * * * * * * ● * * * * * * * * * * *

At the Grand Canyon in Arizona—a fantastic tourist attraction in America—the explorers run into a couple who happened to have visited Africa for the first time in their lives. This sets the stage to highlight uncertainties during explorations.

In their *Coming to Africa* documentary, Dick and Kelly's experiences bring to the forefront some of the challenges one encounters when pursuing dreams in a foreign land.

Ama and Gold Coast Boy can certainly attest to these experiences.

Dick is excited to meet a couple from a country in Africa he and his girlfriend visited in the past for the first time. They instantly become friends in the course of a lunch break on an organized tour of the Grand Canyon and the Hoover Dam.

"Hello, my name is Gold Coast Boy. Please, meet my wife, Ama. We are from Ghana in West Africa", Gold Coast Boy introduces himself and his wife.

"Well, well. I am Kelly from Minnesota and my boy-friend, Dick, is from Iowa," Kelly quickly makes the intro-ductions with great enthusiasm as she and Dick are itching to tell Gold Coast Boy and Ama about their past experiences from their first visit to the continent.

"So, what brings you folks here to America and the Grand Canyon in particular?" Dick inquires.

"In order not to bore you, I will keep it brief but sweet," says Gold Coast Boy.

Ama draws closer to her man.

"Prior to meeting Ama, I have virtually spent decades combing the universe with a toothpick, looking for my childhood friend whom I lost contact with as a result of politically constricted tunnel vision.

"I have been making voyages on four continents in search of him, and here we are in America."

"Oh, wow! Four continents?" Dick asks.

"Ibrahim loves nature, adventure, and sightseeing. The Grand Canyon gives us the hope of finding him, and so here we are at the Grand Canyon," adds Gold Coast Boy.

"We hope you can help us find him," Ama makes a heartfelt appeal to Dick and Kelly.

You should see the sad looks on the faces of Dick and Kelly.

"Sorry to hear about that separation," says Dick who is emotionally touched as he hears the gloomy story.

"Thank you, Dick, but we have not given up the search," declares Gold Coast Boy.

"Kelly and I were in Africa for the very first time about two years ago to take a lifetime dream vacation to the continent we heard so many conflicting and negative stories about that we wanted to paint our own pictures of.

"We stayed at the Movenpick and Kempinski Hotels in Accra for the most part but toured places including the Asesewa International Convention Center and the

Asesewa Biotechnology Center of Excellence, both in the Eastern Region."

Ama and Gold Coast Boy smile as they look at each other's faces while holding hands.

Dick pauses momentarily.

Then Ama says, "You know what? My husband is from Asesewa and he is the founder and Chief Executive Officer of the two businesses you just mentioned.

"Oh, my God. What a small world," Kelly responds and Ama adds, "A small world indeed, and that is an assurance that we have a good chance of finding Ibrahim."

"Amen. Let it be, let it be sooner than next time since next time never comes and procrastination takes no one nowhere," says Gold Coast Boy as he gazes into the sky.

Dick continues to recount their experiences in Ghana.

"While we were at Asesewa, we took the *trotro* [a popular public transportation system in Ghana] for most errands. We barely used taxi or Uber or asked for rides in luxurious vehicles. We did our own grocery shopping for fresh produce from the Asesewa Mall and did our own cooking.

"Some of the children had never seen a white man or woman let alone seen them pound their own *fufu* [a local meal prepared from boiled plantain and cocoyam, cassava with plantain or cassava with cocoyam, for example]. These kids offered to help us, but we politely turned down their offers.

"We also learned and prepared other local meals like *banku* [a meal made from fermented corn dough], okra stew with smoked salmon or tilapia, not to mention the popular *kenkey* [a fermented corn dough product] and fish usually served with *shito* [a hot pepper sauce that jalapeño pepper cannot compete with] plus *kelewele* [seasoned fried ripe plantain]."

"Please, stop, stop here, I beg you. Stop, please. You are making my mouth watery, drooling, and salivating like a starving pig," Gold Coast Boy can no longer bear hearing about these popular delicious Ghanaian dishes.

Everybody laughs.

"Moreover, we took *trotro* to the Akosombo Dam and the Volta Lake besides hiking at the Afadjato Mountain in the Volta Region. We tried learning the local languages, such as Krobo, Ga, Ewe, and Twi, and that helped us quite a bit. We made a lot of friends including the children," Dick adds.

"Really? That is amazing and impressive, you folks," Ama says as she can't believe her ears.

"I tell you Ghanaians are very friendly people and very polite," Dick expresses his appreciation of the citizens they interacted with.

"What we saw on American television before making this trip was totally different from what we experienced onsite. There were humongous, luxurious five-star hotels and business facilities that I could never have imagined seeing in an African country. There were some poor people, though, like you see in every country," Kelly adds.

Dick tells Gold Coast Boy and Ama, "Oh yes, we still have good memories and want to go back to Africa."

"I was just about to ask you if you folks would want to visit Ghana again," Ama remarks.

"They charged everything in U.S. dollars when we were in Accra. Major news broadcasts in Ghana focused on America regularly. We thought we were in an American colony. Every year, Kelly and I saw the New Year's Parade and the New Year's Ball Drop at Times Square in New York City.

"So, that made us think it was no issue celebrating the American 4th of July there. We organized a huge 4th of July Fireworks Celebration party at the Accra Civic Community Center Park to celebrate America's Independence Day. The occasion attracted a big crowd of invited and self-invited people from neighboring cities. We did some grilling of hot dogs, goat meat and snail. We served alcoholic and nonalcoholic beverages.

"The local people did not like the hot dogs because they thought they were made of dog meat. Their favorite items on the menu were the goat meat and the snail. Drinking of fresh palm wine and the locally brewed 90 percent proof high-content alcohol, *akpeteshie*, in the 99-degree Fahrenheit [37.2-degree Celsius] humid weather went on unabated. A few people mixed the whisky with the *akpeteshie*. It proved to be futile especially when consuming this drink or any alcoholic drink on empty stomach.

"Foreigners, a lot of them from the United States, Jamaica, France, Germany, The Netherlands, Italy, Spain and the United Kingdom had no problems doing justice to the hot dogs, Budweiser, Guinness, Heineken, Star Beer, Gulder Lager Beer and an array of wines."

That is not unusual, you think?

In his recollective memory lane, Dick continues, "There were some sporting activities including basketball, American football, football [soccer], baseball, tennis and volleyball. Of course, there was twerk dancing and all sorts of dancing moves to the tunes of rock and roll, highlife, rap music, gospel music, and reggae music.

"Some of the people in the crowd brought and shared drugs at the party but Kelly and I were wrongly accused for allegedly providing drugs to the people.

"A good number of the local media outlets reported that an American couple was arrested for celebrating the American 4th of July festivity in Ghana. This fake news went wild and viral on many social media channels."

"What a memorable experience you folks had," Gold Coast Boy says.

Dick further describes their "first time in Africa" experiences.

"We made a big mistake with the wild party. And we paid dearly for it. We ended up in police detention for forty-eight hours prior to our appearance in court. We were charged with attempting to set the city on fire, public intoxication, playing loud music in public, and importing firecrackers and restricted alcoholic drinks into the country illegally."

"It is sad your cool agenda to celebrate the American Independence Day landed you and Kelly in hot water," Ama says in empathy.

"A crowd of local citizens and foreigners gathered to mount a peaceful demonstration to demand that Kelly and I be set free immediately and with no conditions attached. Despite the fact that we both pleaded guilty, we were each fined to provide to the Mayor of Accra two live goats, two big baskets of snail, and two bottles of *akpeteshie*.

"The American Embassy's and the protesters' interventions paid off. We were finally set free without any bonds or restrictions."

· · · · · · · · · · ● · · · · · · · · · · ·

There are many uncertainties that keep crossing your path as you chase your dreams, but you just don't give up. You've got to keep moving forward tenaciously.

The resilient exploration to find Ibrahim now moves from the Grand Canyon to the State of Georgia.

Their next Chimeric flight takes off to Hartsfield-Jackson International Airport in Atlanta, Georgia and is followed by a road trip in the land-mode navigation from Atlanta to Tifton, Georgia, where Gold Coast Boy reunites with a globally renowned turf grass geneticist and his family whom Gold Coast Boy had met in India in the past.

After enrolling for about two semesters at the local Community College in Tifton, Abraham Baldwin Agricultural College (ABAC), Gold Coast Boy transfers to Iowa State University (ISU) in Ames, Iowa. He lives in Ankeny and commutes to Ames.

Not long after he arrives in Iowa, the airwaves are filled with another controversial deportation order swirling in the global social news media.

This time, Nigeria expels Ghanaians apparently in retaliation for Nigerians who were exiled from Ghana during the days of HY's political intolerance that marked the genesis of Ibrahim's loss of contact with his childhood friend.

· · · · · · ● ● ● ● ● ● ● ● ● ● ● · · · ·

On a hot, sticky, humid 101-degree Fahrenheit (38.3-degree Celsius) Iowa summer day, Gold Coast Boy gets a hint from Manny Kojokutu, an African friend at ISU suggesting that the best place he could find his friend would be in the corn fields during the summer break.

Many African students engage in the extremely tedious but highly paid contract manual corn detasseling or emasculation where mechanical detasseling may not be available or feasible. This method of controlling pollination or fertilization involves designated immature tassels (*male reproductive organs*) removal prior to their shedding of pollen grains that pollinate the silks (*female reproductive organs*) of desired corn plants.

Gold Coast Boy and Ama are convinced that this would definitely be the place to find Ibrahim.

Right after Manny's regular day's work at ISU, they decide to ride with him to the vast cornfields in Ekow-

Dennis County which is forty-five minutes' drive west of Ames.

At the end of the detasseling job around nine o'clock at night, the sun is still up and embellished with a charming array of the tantalizing colors of the rainbow. As the trio drive back to campus, they run into a van carrying five African students.

With the distraction caused by the rainbow, the old Nissan Model 3 van hits a deer and the front tire comes off and deflates. The commuters stand desolate not knowing what to do because they have neither a spare tire nor a mobile phone to call a towing company for help.

Luckily for them, Manny Kojokutu shows up with a spare tire for the same-age Nissan van. While the van's tire is being replaced, Gold Coast Boy jumps at the occasion to inform the group about his long-lost friend from Ghana called Ibrahim and his long-term commitment to finding him.

No sooner has Gold Coast Boy finished narrating his story than Andy Rexford tells Gold Coast Boy, "Ibrahim and I have been good friends for the past few years. He transferred from ISU to Drake University in Des Moines, a few miles away from Ames, where the Iowa State University main campus is."

After Andy gives a description that perfectly matches that of Ibrahim, Gold Coast Boy and Ama are filled with delight and the thought that the end of their search is going to be in Iowa. His resounding description vividly clears every doubt in the minds of Ama and Gold Coast Boy.

Niifio Annan overhears Andy's story but keeps quiet. Back at the Corn Dog Residence Hall at ISU's main campus, he tells Gold Coast Boy "Andy was lying to you. He got those perfect descriptions from a video we watched together on the internet from a social media channel called WAM that is owned by one Nina Willie in the United Kingdom. Ibrahim never attended Iowa State University. If by some fate you find Ibrahim at Drake University, it is a rare soothsayer's fairy tale," Niifio claims.

Confusion causes a wave of storms in Gold Coast Boy's mind. Andy's descriptions are a perfect match while Niifio's revelations seem to bring out the gospel truth. Niifio's divine disclosure momentarily evaporates the faith in Gold Coast Boy subsequent to the stories of the two good friends, Andy and Niifio.

· · · · · · · · · ● ● · · · · · · · · ·

The truth is that neither Andy nor Niifio ever knew Ibrahim. The gospel truth unknown to millions of people on the planet (including Gold Coast Boy and Ama) is that Ibrahim gained admission to Drake University to do his PharmD and LLM studies after completing his BPharm degree at Grinnell College in Grinnell, Iowa.

· · · · · · · · ● ● ● ◉ ● ● ● ● ● · · · · · ·

Ama asks Gold Coast Boy not to despair. "I know you. You have a faith stronger than the bamboo tree in the virgin African rainforest," she revives his credence as she gently rubs her charming cheeks on his face.

"We shall go to Drake and search for him no matter the circumstances," Ama says with contagious enthusiasm.

In the air-navigation mode, they take off in Chimeric from their Ankeny, Iowa, township to the popular annual Drake Relays athletic event on a beautiful Saturday.

Bob Bensons, an Iowa City *hometown boy* and a popular athlete of The University of Iowa (alias Iowa), who is most affectionately called Suru Lere, had been the record holder of the 100-meter, 200-meter, 4 x 100-meter, 4 x 200-meter, and 400-meter events in the history of the Drake Relays.

For this enviable achievement, he has been recognized with a modern sports facility, the Suru Lere Sports Stadium. Furthermore, the Ham and Tall Corn Fraternity cum Sorority House has been named after him for being the most famous student in the history of the College of Agriculture.

That was then. Wait until he is faced squarely by the unknown Ibrahim from Drake University, an archrival of The University of Iowa.

Suru Lere, though, had never set all these records in one meeting.

Gold Coast Boy being a mile runner in high school and a soccer star in elementary school, never misses watching the enchanting athletic events at the Drake Relays which draw spectators and athletes of all ages from the United States of America and abroad.

On that Saturday, Ibrahim happens to be competing in the five events. What are the chances of picking a day to watch the weeklong Drake Relays on the day Ibrahim will be participating?

Guess what? Ama, Gold Coast Boy and Ibrahim may have crisscrossed one another's paths in the past without knowing it.

The couple has been in attendance for a couple of years. This year's is special and memorable, so they think, in the sense that it promises the fulfillment of years of dreams and a deliciously sumptuous yet tumultuous realization of their contemplations of finding a long-lost friend for whom they have been coming up with various composite drawings.

No guarantees though. It can happen in America or anywhere on earth.

Ibrahim's name on his jersey quickly gets Gold Coast Boy's curious attention.

"Man! Other than the well-known computer company called IBM, there aren't many people or anything called IBM on this planet. It's got to be him. This has got to be him," Gold Coast Boy reassures Ama.

The *Big Adults Relay* in which Ibrahim is featured also inspires the duo that this must be their friend due to his age and the age category of the participants.

· · · · · · ● ● ● ● ● ◉ ● ● ● ● · · · · ·

The events announcer broadcasts the start of the 200-meter race.

In this tensed and highly charged moment, Suru Lere makes a brilliant and intimidating take off. Running at a good pace, he leads the event's participants three-quarters of the way through the race. Then Ibrahim comes from behind to overtake Suru Lere who is favored to win. He is shocked, nearly passes out and ends up in fourth place with Ibrahim winning his first race in a record time. Ibrahim raises the eye brows of many athletes, spectators and his own as he is unknown in the history of the annual events.

Suru Lere and his Iowa team win the 4 x 100 meters relay in a record time. This boosts the team's supremacy in the Drake Relays and hopes of collecting several gold medals at the end of the season's meeting. Coming in the second place is an unheard of team, The Technical University College of Business Innovations and Biodynamics from Australia, led by Evans Johnston. Ibrahim and his Drake University team end up third.

The 4 x 400-meter relay sees Suru Lere run in the first leg. He puts the Iowa squad in a very comfortable lead. The University of Iowa is still in the lead after the third lap.

The fourth and final lap features Ibrahim. He steadily closes the gap established by Suru Lere. The stadium roars like a zoo filled with lions, gorillas, polar bears, and tigers demonstrating their loneliness due to the two-legged tourists' absence from their kingdoms since the IED-imposed lockdowns, solitary confinements and restrictions on people, business operations, and travel.

By a few split seconds, Ibrahim and his team win the 4 x 400-meter relay in record time. Iowa fans get agitated and start throwing garbage, hot dogs and pig waste on the racetrack.

The rest of the evening is even more tense. Iowa loses the 4 x 200-meter relay to Ibrahim and his Drake quartet. In the 400 meters clash, Suru Lere is no contest at all to Ibrahim who wins this event in record time flying like a jet.

Now comes the final event of the season—the 100-meter dash. This is Suru Lere's final chance to prove his superiority over Ibrahim. Drake stadium becomes the noisiest ever in the history of the athletics meetings.

All eight athletes from various geographical zones take their lanes and are poised for glory. Ibrahim, Suru Lere and Evans are in lanes 5, 6 and 8, respectively. Each athlete looks extremely self-confident, and it is anybody's chance to win this event.

The event's plastic gun fires corn kernel bullets to signal the start of the race.

Panorama from Ecuador in lane 1 makes a false start. A second lineup is set following repeated warnings about the rules for the event which state that an athlete caught in false start for the third time will be automatically disqualified.

At the start of the second chance, Santiago from Chile in lane 7 makes a false start.

The event now gets tenser than ever. The whole stadium is filled with anxiety and uproar. The athlete in lane 4, VonDoe of Germany, also makes a false start.

The race finally takes off successfully the fourth time. Panorama takes the lead for the first twenty meters of the race. He is quickly overtaken by Suru Lere with Ibrahim closely following Suru Lere in third place. Ibrahim shortly gets in the lead with fifteen meters to the finish line.

Simon from Greece in lane 3 overtakes Ibrahim but is momentarily surpassed by Suru Lere who gets beaten by Ibrahim at the finish line in a head-to-head photo finish. Five repetitions of the video camera replay are needed to declare Ibrahim the winner of the 100-meter dash in another record time.

Ibrahim sweeps all the gold medals in five events—200-meters dash, 4 X 200 meters, 4 X 400 meters, 400 meters dash and 100 meters dash—in brand-new record times. His winning spree and record-shattering performances sumptuously decorate the icing on the cake.

Breaking of all five records in one meeting turns the Drake University Stadium that evening into a blend of ecstasy and melancholy never seen before.

Suru Lere, his coaching staff, and the fans of The University of Iowa challenge all the five defeats and demand that Ibrahim be subjected to a series of drug tests, which he has no qualms about.

Thanks to advancements in innovative technologies, no trace of drugs is detected in Ibrahim's test samples following the rapid, sensitive and specific tests performed. The test results come as a surprise for Suru Lere, his coaching staff and fans.

Ibrahim is acknowledged the newly crowned best-ever Drake Relays athlete. This achievement paves the way for Gold Coast Boy to strike up a long-awaited conversation. He and Ama rush to the athletics field.

Pretending to be a television sports journalist holding a microphone, wearing a hat and a jacket labeled GBC-ONE TV, Gold Coast Boy walks up to Ibrahim at the end of the 100-meter event which happens to mark the end of the year's athletic festivities.

"Hey, mister Ibrahim, congratulations on your performances which are not of nanoscopic, microscopic or diminutive value but of immaculate pride of Africa," says

Gold Coast Boy with a smile the width of the Atlantic Ocean. Ibrahim embraces him with a big hug.

"Pride of Africa? How do you know that I am from Africa?" Ibrahim asks.

"From the distinguishing shape of your forehead," Gold Coast Boy replies with a giggle and they both laughed out loud (lol).

"By the way, Ibrahim, if I may ask, did you ever live in Ghana?" Ibrahim responds by asking Gold Coast Boy, "By the way, are you representing Ghana Broadcasting Corporation Television Station in Accra, Ghana?"

You can imagine the look on their faces as they both laugh.

"Are you running for or being sponsored by the computer company called IBM? Is IBM on your jersey an abbreviation of your name, Ibrahim Mahamadose?"

Ibrahim quickly answers, "You must have read about me somewhere or do you know me?"

Gold Coast Boy repeats, "Did you ever live in Ghana?"

"Yes, I used to live in Ghana. I was born in Ghana of Nigerian ..."

Gold Coast Boy interrupts him and finishes the sentence for Ibrahim by saying: "Nigerian parents who lived at a town in the Eastern Region called... Asesewa!" They say the last word in harmony to the joy and admiration of the spectators.

"I am Tettey Apotsi-Batsa but I am fondly called by my friends, the ..."

"The Gold Coast ... Boy"

Again, they both respond spontaneously with an emotional elation.

"Wow! We are in a world as little as the tiniest toe-nail of a rabbit-nosed yellow baby squirrel.

"So many years," Gold Coast Boy.

"I know."

"Where have you been, my friend?" each of them asks concurrently.

"Hmmmmm. You know, the Help Yourself politicians were to blame, Gold Coast Boy. The HY leaders those days had a perpetual incurable political myopia. They blamed foreigners for the lack of jobs, an embarrassing educational system, lack of affordable healthcare, the housing shortage, devastatingly dangerous roads, and the high inflation rate in the country."

"There was a chronic economic mess," Gold Coast Boy contributes to the recollection.

"The world needs ethical politics and politicians who are sensitive to the needs of those who vote them into office not politicians who are dying of knowledge starvation and malnutrition," says Ibrahim.

This reminiscence from their youthful days still echoes from the bottom of their hearts.

· · · · · · · · ● ◉ ● · · · · · · · · · ·

"Gold Coast Boy, you have really redefined friend-ship beyond any and all walls or landscapes. You went combing every corner of the universe in search of me on four continents, starting from Africa, going through Europe to Asia and North America, and then back to Africa.

"Here, my true friend, I honor you with my 4 x 200-meter relay gold medal which is an emblem of oneness, a team, a family, and one world. It also signifies the value of being there for one another, being one anoth-er's brother's keeper or one another's sister's keeper."

"This gesture of awarding me with your 4 x 200-meter relay gold medal will remain golden in my heart forever, Ibrahim. I lack words to express my appreciation to you."

Turning to the crowd, Gold Coast Boy goes on: "And to you all the people whose paths we crisscrossed at one point or another, never forget that you have profoundly impacted the course of my pilgrimage and reshaped my life in many ways.

"In the long run, I hold dear to my heart all the seconds, minutes, hours and instances we shared together no matter how diminutive the circumstances throughout the decades of my explorations. You all, beyond doubt, have secured a special abode in my heart."

Talking about one another's sisters, Gold Coast Boy beckons Ama, "Please, come on down and meet the gentleman we have been combing the planet for, the one and only Ibrahim Mahamadose."

With all the excitement from this climax resonating from the center of his heart, Gold Coast Boy goes, "Ibrahim, meet my lovely, caring wife and manager, Ama."

With arms as wide as the wings of the giant red hawk and the beaming smile of the sun rising amicably in the east, Ama gives Ibrahim the biggest hug of his life.

Ibrahim loses his bearings shortly following this once-in-a-lifetime hug.

Directing attention to Gold Coast Boy, Ibrahim says, "You epitomize the ethos of resilient tenacity, sustainable faith, and humility by trailblazing wherever you go and in whatever you do.

"You have demonstrated that humanity is capable of fulfilling promises and accomplishing dreams no matter how excruciating the circumstances may be.

"I am so proud of you. No amount of words or combination of the letters of the alphabet can describe my gratitude to you to any degree of precision.

"May God bless you, my true friend, real friend. May God continue to shower you with His blessings. May you live twice the longevity of the African baobab tree so you can touch many more souls."

Tears continue flying out the eyes of the reunited friends just like hot summer water skating down the rocks of the Boti waterfalls near Huhunya.

· · · · · · · · · ● ● ● ● ● ● ● · · · · ·

BRIDGES, WALLS AND THE BOOMERANG

"The passion for cherishing one another builds bridges connecting all corners of the universe. Burning bridges only makes the world's problems more dreadful.

"The consistency in inculcating the spirit of brotherly and sisterly love is a sustainable means of building the momentum towards achieving peace and harmony on earth. Let us all endeavor not to falter in showing love and care for one another," Nina says.

"Illegal and unethical deportation of people to known and unknown lands show that humankind is out of touch with humility to the extent of making even the Stone Age seem more humane.

"Building walls, fences or barricades around the borders of various nations or regions and closing borders for the joy of it shall eventually crumble the fundamental cores of humanity and democracy and they shall be extinct," Ibrahim adds.

In further supporting Ibrahim, Ama says, "Closing borders to prevent the spread of lethal pandemic diseases and for national security or sovereignty can go a long way in sustaining global health, population and economic stability.

"Travel to tourist attraction centers is educational and worth experiencing in the absence of any wars and worldwide disease threats such as in the case of IED World *War III* which Professor Lilian Lomo-Jones, founder of the Ghana Religious and Biotechnology Society [GRABS] predicts will end two years after its inception.

"The IED global civil war can enlighten the poor, vulnerable and afflicted to the realization that:

> ➢ we are equal in the presence of the creator of humankind and all creatures
> ➢ we are each other's keepers
> ➢ no matter a person's immigration status, national origin, cultural IQ, economic, social or educational status, we are all accountable to God, first and foremost."

"Friendship is a boomerang. Friends can change, go away, or vanish into the wilderness but they will eventually find you. Hold on to your dreams and friends all through the ages no matter what the circumstances may be.

"Regardless of how long, winding and land mine-filled your journey may be, you will definitely get there if you make the effort religiously to move one step after the other. Great things in life's journey come with tenaciously greater hard work. Cry out loudly [col], cry out softly or silently [cos] but cries vibrate walls to open doors to amazing rewards," Gold Coast Boy brings down the curtain.

· · · · · · ● ● ● ● ◉ ● ● ● ● · · · · ·

"May I make a suggestion, guys? Ama asks, touched by the heart of an angelic sleeping baby.

"I think we should go and celebrate this enormous triumph in Africa—Ghana, to be precise. Let's go to modern Ghana, a country which now has an agenda to cure the chronic political shortsightedness.

"Our parents, relatives, and friends are all still alive and will be witnesses to this great life-changing experience."

Gold Coast Boy and Ibrahim concur.

"Yeah, great idea, Ama!" they both say in resonance.

· · · · · · · · ● · · · · · · · · ·

"Let's go! *Allons-y! Vamonos! Mu je!*" all three exclaim while boarding Chimeric-79-GH, singing J & O's signature lyrics "Tena, tena, tenacious" and jumping with their hands pointing to heaven.

· · · · · · · · ● · · · · · · · · ·

WORDS OF WISDOM

John F. Kennedy

"**C**hange is the law of life. And those who look only to the past or present are certain to miss the future." John F. Kennedy Quotes. (n.d.). BrainyQuote. com. Retrieved on September 10, 2019 from BrainyQuote. com Web site: https://www.brainyquote.com/quotes/ john_f_kennedy_121068

Nelson Mandela

"If you talk to a man in a language he understands, that goes to his head. If you talk to him in his language, that goes to his heart." Retrieved on December 5, 2018 from:

https://www.goodreads.com/author/ quotes/367338.Nelson_Mandela

ACKNOWLEDGMENTS

Mr. Philip Stinard of blessed memory is greatly and sincerely appreciated. Adhering to time-sensitive deadlines, he made relentless efforts to review this manuscript. He also provided suggestions not of miniature values but of tremendous imagination. A distinguished Maize Genetics and Genomics Database (MaizeGDB) curator, he demonstrated that you don't have to have a doctoral degree to be a famous scientist.

This book would not have come to fruition without the innovative knowledge imparted by Dr. Donald S. Robertson (a future Nobel Prize winner), the late world-renowned geneticist, professor, and discoverer of the Robertson Maize Mutator Element (MuDR/ Mu Transposable Element). He is greatly recognized for giving me the opportunity to work in his Corn Genetics Laboratory (Genetics Lab) and for teaching me firsthand during all my undergraduate years. He also enabled me to co-author with him my three undergraduate research papers in the Maize Genetics Cooperation Newsletter (now curated in the Maize Genetics and Genomics Database-MaizeGDB).

Dr. Benny White, a greatly respected mentor and professor is sincerely acknowledged for motivating the writing of this book, like other inspiring people never to be forgotten.

Similarly, Mr. Faustin Kofi Aklenam Klaye, a renowned historian who was my teacher and athletics coach when I was in high school, is highly valued for his remarkable mentoring.

Dr. Shadrack and Dr. Linda Okiror are treasured for their esteemed mentorships for decades and motivations over the years which contributed to inspiring the writing of this book for the world to know that dreams can, indeed, be transformed into reality.

Finally, a heartfelt gratitude goes to Sylvia Mallet for contributing immensely to the reviewing and formatting of the manuscript

FURTHER KNOWLEDGE-BUILDING RESOURCES

1944: Jumping Genes. National Human Genome Research Institute. Retrieved on September 29, 2020 from: https://www.genome.gov/25520251/online-education-kit-1944-jumping-genes

Intermittent Explosive Disorder. Cleveland Clinic. Retrieved on August 25, 2020 from https://www.mayoclinic.org/diseases-conditions/intermittent-explosive-disorder/symptoms-causes/syc-20373921

Pioneers of revolutionary CRISPR gene editing win chemistry Nobel. Retrieved on October 09, 2020 from https://www.nature.com/articles/d41586-020-02765-9

The Mutator Transposable Element System of Maize.
Retrieved on September 29, 2020 from:
https://link.springer.com/chapter/10.
1007%2F978-3-642-79795-8_9

What are the ethical concerns of genome editing? Retrieved on July 4, 2020 from:
https://www.genome.gov/about-genomics/
policy-issues/Genome-Editing/ethical-concerns